BREAKING DOWN FITZGERALD

HELEN M. TURNER

JB JOSSEY-BASS™
A Wiley Brand

Published by John Wiley & Sons, Inc., Hoboken, New Jersey.

Published simultaneously in Canada.

For general information on our other products and services or for technical support, please contact our Customer Care Department within the United States at (800) 762-2974, outside the United States at (317) 572-3993 or fax (317) 572-4002.

Wiley also publishes its books in a variety of electronic formats. Some content that appears in print may not be available in electronic formats. For more information about Wiley products, visit our web site at www.wiley.com.

For general information on our other products and services or for technical support, please contact our Customer Care Department within the United States at (800) 762-2974, outside the United States at (317) 572-3993 or fax (317) 572-4002.

Wiley also publishes its books in a variety of electronic formats. Some content that appears in print may not be available in electronic formats. For more information about Wiley products, visit our web site at www.wiley.com.

Library of Congress Cataloging-in-Publication Data is Available:

ISBNs: 9781119805328 (paperback),
9781119805335 (epub),
9781119805342 (ePDF)

COVER ART & DESIGN: PAUL MCCARTHY

SKY10032201_122821

Contents

Breaking Down Fitzgerald: Introduction

This guide to F. Scott Fitzgerald has three key purposes. The first is to explore his most famous and most widely studied novel, *The Great Gatsby* (1925). Detailed consideration is given to the novel's composition, motifs, themes, and characters. The second purpose is to engage with other aspects of Fitzgerald's life and work. By contextualizing the text in this manner, students will deepen their understanding and appreciation of the novel. The third goal of this guide is to garner wider interest in Fitzgerald. The majority of students encounter the author for the first time through his most famous novel, but unfortunately, this can also be where engagement with Fitzgerald ends. However, he was a writer for a period of more than twenty years, and during that time he wrote three additional complete novels and an unfinished one, close to two hundred short stories, as well as dozens of essays and magazine articles.

The structure of the book is as follows:

- Chapter One provides an overview of Fitzgerald's life, the details of which read like a novel in themselves.

- The second chapter is concerned with important cultural and literary contexts that influenced the writer and his work.

- Chapter Three is focused on Fitzgerald's first two novels, *This Side of Paradise* (1920) and *The Beautiful and Damned* (1922).

- Chapter Four is the longest in the book as it is focused on *The Great Gatsby* (1925). Consideration is given to its composition, major characters, and motifs as well as structure and themes.

- In Chapter Five attention turns to Fitzgerald's later novels, *Tender Is the Night* (1934) and *The Last Tycoon* (1941).
- The final chapter is concerned with the author's short stories and essays.

At the end of each chapter are details for further reading but also further viewing and listening, which opens up Fitzgerald's work and world through a variety of resources in different media.

Before turning attention to the man and his work, it is worth pondering the question: why Fitzgerald? In recent decades there has been a reconsideration of the literary canon. Who is included in the western literary tradition, who has been excluded and—importantly—why? Traditionally it has privileged the narratives of dead white men at the expense of the voices of others. So, does this particular dead white man have something valuable to tell the modern reader? Some of the attitudes he expresses in his fiction and in personal correspondence seem out of step with contemporary values. His depiction of race, gender, and sexuality can at times rely on crude stereotypes. For example, it is impossible to see Meyer Wolfshiem as anything other than a caricature of anti-Semitic tropes. Many critics have raised concerns about Fitzgerald's depiction of women as they are simultaneously infantilized and held responsible for the frustrations and disappointments of men. His descriptions of black people lack depth and agency.

However, through a close reading of his work, it is possible to see that Fitzgerald's response to a changing world is complex. He inherited the beliefs and attitudes of a Victorian world. However, in the aftermath of the First World War, assumptions about gender, race, and sexuality that previously appeared "correct" or "normal" were brought into question. In his work it is evident that he is wrestling with these changing attitudes, creating ambivalence and at times apparent agreement with both progressive and reactionary views. His description of "three modish negroes, two bucks and a girl" that made Nick laugh "aloud as the yolks of their eyeballs rolled towards us in haughty rivalry" (Fitzgerald 2019, p. 83) is countered with Nick's recognition of there being "something pathetic in his [Tom's] concentration, as if his complacency, more acute than of old, was not enough to him any more" as Tom attempts to explain his racist theories regarding the collapse of civilization (p. 17).

Fitzgerald was living in a frantic, changing world: a world contending with the aftermath of war, changing social relationships between men and women, bans on alcohol and illicit boozing, new media and entertainment, and a flu pandemic that killed millions. In many respects, it was a time not unlike our own where certainty seems like a concept that will never return. People are bombarded with contrary attitudes and opinions toward sexuality, gender identity, climate change, and public health. There is something familiar in Fitzgerald's life and work in terms of mood if not in the exact detail. He explores the anxieties and excitement of change that we can all understand. He certainly does have something to tell the modern reader.

Chapter 1
Fitzgerald's Life

F. Scott Fitzgerald's life has garnered almost as much interest as his most famous novel. At the beginning of his career in the 1920s, he went through extraordinary highs at a time when fame combined with mass media to create celebrity culture. He was talked about in newspapers and magazines as the spokesman of his generation. It was also at this time that the image—both still and moving—became ubiquitous. His good looks and those of his glamorous wife, Zelda, made them an early incarnation of the celebrity couple. The highs could not last, however, and the desperate predicaments that both of them would find themselves in through the course of the 1930s read like a tragedy. He would die in 1940 in Hollywood, aged only forty-four, but his life began in the Midwest city of St. Paul, Minnesota.

CHILDHOOD AND PRINCETON (1896–1917)

In the popular imagination, F. Scott Fitzgerald is associated with the glamour of New York and the French Riviera in the 1920s, but his roots were firmly planted in the turn of the century Midwest. He was born on September 24, 1896, in St. Paul, Minnesota, to Edward and Mollie Fitzgerald. The couple represented two alternative traditions of American identity. His maternal line was immigrant Irish; his grandfather had arrived as a child in the United States in the 1840s. Through industry and identifying valuable opportunities, Philip McQuillan amassed a considerable fortune running a wholesale grocery business that would be the income source Fitzgerald's family relied upon through much of his childhood. This financial reliance was the result of Edward owning and then losing a furniture business in 1898 that led to a family move to Buffalo, New York, for employment. This work with Procter & Gamble ended in 1908 and a return to the Midwest and financial dependency followed.

Edward's background contrasted with his wife's in a number of significant ways. He was born in Maryland into a well-established Southern family whose influence had faded. At the end of the Civil War, Edward had headed north and west, eventually settling in industrial St. Paul, home of railroad magnate James J. Hill. The pull between the self-made and reinvented idea of American identity and the allure of inherited wealth and social influence his parents represented reveals itself as a tension both in Fitzgerald's life and in his writing.

Throughout his great success in the 1920s, Fitzgerald showed little appreciation for the role his parents had played in the formation of his talent. Remarks about them during this time are either disparaging or pitying. However, Edward was central in passing on a love of literature, particularly in the form of English Romanticism. Fitzgerald's lifelong love of Byron and John Keats specifically can be traced to the influence of his father. He applied a less flattering acknowledgement to his mother, claiming that weaknesses in his character were a direct result of her overindulgence of him in childhood. Her behavior was not entirely surprising when we reflect on the fact that the Fitzgeralds buried three of Scott's siblings in infancy.

Fitzgerald's interest in writing revealed itself early on and a number of his short stories were published in school magazines, first, at the St. Paul Academy, which Fitzgerald attended between 1908 and 1911, and subsequently at the Newman School, where he was a student until 1913. The second institution was vital in Fitzgerald's emotional and creative development as it was here that he met Monsignor Sigourney Fay, who encouraged his artistic leanings. The friendship between the two also led to Fitzgerald flirting with the idea of the priesthood. Fitzgerald would use him as a model for the character Monsignor Darcy in his first novel, *This Side of Paradise* (1920).

Although Fitzgerald was already showing signs of writerly talent by adding playwriting to his short story accomplishments, he did not particularly shine academically. However, university was an expected path for a man of his class to follow and he set his heart on the Ivy League and Princeton. His maternal grandmother's timely death meant that the tuition fees could be met and the threat of the University of Minnesota to save money was removed (Bruccoli 2002, p. 37).

Fitzgerald's time at Princeton was no more academically successful than his school days. However, he made a number of important friends during his time as an undergraduate, including the poet John Peal Bishop, the writer and critic Edmund Wilson, and John Biggs, future judge and—on Fitzgerald's death—executor of his estate. Fitzgerald carried on writing and performing with the university's Triangle Club, as well as contributing to the university magazines *Tiger* and *Nassau Literary Magazine* that both Wilson and Bishop were heavily involved in. These creative outlets were the focus of his attention rather than his studies.

The outcome of his haphazard approach to academia was that in 1916, he returned to Princeton to repeat his junior year. By the beginning of the following year, he was making little progress and had little chance of graduating. In April 1917, the United States entered the war, relieving Fitzgerald of having to admit his academic failure or make decisions about his immediate future. By October, he was a commissioned second lieutenant in the infantry stationed at Fort Leavenworth, Kansas. The following March he was at Fort Sheridan near Montgomery, Alabama, and had been promoted to first lieutenant. Fitzgerald would not take part in the action of the First World War, which he recognized as the defining experience of his generation, but he was about to experience a life-changing moment of a different kind. For it was here in Montgomery that he would meet eighteen-year-old Zelda Sayre, his future wife.

MEETING ZELDA AND EARLY SUCCESS (1918–1924)

Before his arrival at Fort Sheridan, Fitzgerald had already begun work on the novel that would eventually become *This Side of Paradise* and an early draft was completed by February 1918. It was submitted to Charles Scribner's Sons publishing house in New York for consideration under the title *The Romantic Egotist,* but it was rejected in both August and October of that year.

In July, Fitzgerald met Zelda Sayre at a country club dance in Montgomery. She was beautiful, vivacious, and popular; Fitzgerald was besotted. The path to marriage, however, was not without interruption as Zelda was unable to fully commit to Fitzgerald until she was certain that he could provide for her properly. A handsome soldier and would-be writer may have had romantic appeal but Zelda, like all women of her class at this time (as well as Fitzgerald's female characters), needed to be practical too. With no means of generating an income for themselves because of the limited opportunities open to them, women needed to take the decision to marry with both the head and the heart. Her lack of faith at this point in the relationship cast a shadow over their marriage that Fitzgerald could never quite escape.

In 1919, having never seen action overseas, Fitzgerald was dismissed from the army. Intent on marrying Zelda, he headed to New York and a role in advertising. He continued to write and submitted a number of short stories to magazines for publication but was unsuccessful. In June, Zelda—unconvinced that Fitzgerald would make a success of his chosen career and conscious that he had no independent wealth—broke their engagement. Fitzgerald was heartbroken but it triggered a series of events that would set him on the path to fame and fortune. He quit his job in advertising, packed his belongings, and once again returned to St. Paul where in the attic of his parents' home he redrafted his novel in a flurry of activity over the summer months.

In September, Fitzgerald's career as a commercial writer began when *The Smart Set* magazine accepted "Babes in the Woods" for publication. More good news would follow that month when Scribner's editor Maxwell Perkins accepted the newly renamed *This Side of Paradise* for publication. The title came from a poem titled "Tiare Tahiti" (1915) by English poet Rupert Brooke, who had perished during the war. The relationship between Perkins and Fitzgerald would be a mainstay of the author's life. Perkins was not only an extraordinary editor; he was also a loyal and remarkable friend who supported Fitzgerald through some of the darkest periods of his life.

Two months later, another professional contact would enter his life and remain a source of emotional, creative, and financial support. Harold Ober was a literary agent who was working for the Paul Revere Reynolds Agency, which specialized in placing short stories in magazines.[1] Throughout his lifetime, commercial short stories would be the most reliable income stream for Fitzgerald. Almost as soon as the author signed with the agency, Ober sold his story "Head and Shoulders" to *The Saturday Evening Post*, which was one of the most widely read periodicals in the country. It was the beginning of a productive relationship between author and publication that was closely guarded by Ober himself. Over the following months into 1920, a series of Fitzgerald stories was sold to a number of magazines.

On a personal level, things were also on the up. The engagement between Zelda and Fitzgerald resumed in January 1920, as the author's career began to take shape. Within a few months Fitzgerald found himself a published author when *This Side of Paradise* was published on March 26. The first print run of 3,000 copies priced at $1.75 sold out in an astonishing three days and it went on to sell close to 50,000 copies. Just over a week after publication, on April 3, Fitzgerald and Zelda married in a low-key ceremony in the rectory of St. Patrick's Cathedral, New York. Fitzgerald found himself newly married, newly rich, and newly famous. The couple embraced their new life and the freedom that money brought. Parties and excessive drinking were routine. Toward the middle of the year, they rented a house in Westport, Connecticut, where Fitzgerald hoped he would be more productive; it was here that he started his next novel *The Beautiful and Damned* (1922) that drew heavily on the early days of the Fitzgeralds' marriage.

Over the next few years, the couple moved regularly with periods spent in St. Paul, New York, and finally Great Neck on Long Island. Despite their somewhat chaotic lives, Fitzgerald published a number of his most significant short stories during this time, such as "May Day" (1920) and "Bernice Bobs Her Hair" (1920), as well as "The Diamond as Big as The Ritz" and "Winter Dreams," both published in 1922. A collection of stories appeared in 1920 titled *Flappers and Philosophers* followed by *Tales of the Jazz Age* (1922). A third collection of stories would appear more than a decade later, titled *Taps at Reveille* (1935). However, *The Beautiful and Damned*'s publication in 1922 did not have the same impact either commercially or critically as its predecessor. In the midst of the writing and the partying, the couple's only child—a girl—was born on October

---

[1] Harold Ober established his own agency in 1929 and Fitzgerald went with him.

26, 1921, and named for her father: Frances Scott Fitzgerald. She went by Scottie throughout her life. During this period Fitzgerald returned to his previous love of the theatre by writing a play, *The Vegetable* (1923); however, it failed to impress during a pre-Broadway run in Atlantic City and, although published, it has garnered little attention from scholars.

This period of early success is also marked by the beginning of a problem that would haunt Fitzgerald throughout the remainder of his life and contribute considerably to his death, namely his alcoholism. His heavy drinking probably became a physical and psychological addiction by his mid-twenties at the latest. It interfered with Fitzgerald's work patterns as did Zelda's need for amusement. An intelligent and curious woman, her need for interests outside of her marriage saw her eventually turning toward artistic pursuits of her own. Alongside writing herself she would—at different times in her life—also explore ballet and painting.

By 1924, Fitzgerald was desperate to break the cycle of having to write short stories to sell them in order to fund a lifestyle that was indulgent and financially reckless. In an attempt to save money, the couple decided to take advantage of the dollar-franc exchange rate and spend time in Europe. The goal was that Fitzgerald could work uninterrupted on his next novel. Therefore, in the middle of April 1924, the Fitzgeralds were ready to set sail to France and new adventures.

THE GREAT GATSBY AND EUROPEAN TRAVELS (1924–1931)

After their transatlantic crossing, the Fitzgeralds spent just over a week in Paris where they found a suitable nanny for Scottie before heading down to the Riviera. By June they were settled in the Villa Marie in St Raphaël. Fitzgerald began in earnest the writing of his next novel, which he hoped would be a considerable departure from his commercial fiction and would be sustained by a developed artistic vision. Writing to Max Perkins shortly before their departure to Europe, Fitzgerald reflected on the time that he had wasted in the previous two years. He also articulated his hopes for his new book. It was not to be concerned with "trashy imaginings as in my stories but the sustained imagination of a sincere and yet radiant world. So I tread slowly and carefully + at times in considerable distress. The book will be a consciously artistic achievment [sic] + must depend on that as the 1st books did not" (Fitzgerald 1994, p. 67).

Through the summer months Fitzgerald worked on his novel and Zelda was largely left to her own devices, often spending time at the beach sunbathing and swimming in the beautiful Mediterranean Sea. During July, she became involved with a French aviator by the name of Edouard Jozan. The exact nature of the relationship between the two is unknown, with Jozan claiming after the deaths of both Fitzgeralds that it was an innocent flirtation. However—whatever the truth—it introduced a wedge between husband and wife which, some biographers have argued, was never fully repaired. Curiously, it was also a traumatic event that both of them drew upon and reimagined—not only in their fiction—but as an ever-evolving story that the couple shared with friends.

During this period, the Fitzgeralds met Sara and Gerald Murphy, a glamorous and well-connected couple who were noted for their exquisite entertaining as well as their artistic group of friends that included Pablo Picasso, Cole Porter, and Jean Cocteau. They would remain friends and frequent correspondents of Fitzgerald for the rest of his life, despite his drunken antics sometimes putting pressure on his relationships with the Murphys and others.

Fitzgerald spent the remainder of 1924 and the early months of 1925 revising the galley proofs of his novel, which after a series of name changes was now called *The Great Gatsby*. Much of this work was undertaken in Italy, where the Fitzgeralds spent a number of months in both Rome and Capri. During the process he was in regular contact with his editor, Max Perkins, at Scribner's. In a letter dated October 10, 1924, Fitzgerald wrote to him about an upcoming writer that he had heard of but (up to that point) had not met but believed he would be a good fit for Perkins's editorship. "This is to tell you about a young man named Ernest Hemmingway [sic], who lives in Paris, (an American) writes for the Transatlantic Review + has a brilliant future . . . I'd look him up right away. He's the real thing" (Fitzgerald 1994, p. 82).

On April 10, 1925, *The Great Gatsby* was published. Now widely hailed as one of the greatest novels of the twentieth century, at the time of its publication its significance was missed by the book-buying public and it had a critical reception that was mixed at best. The initial print run was 20,870 copies priced at $2.00. In August, an additional 3,000 copies were printed, some of which "were still in Scribner's warehouse when Fitzgerald died" (Bruccoli 2002, p. 217). Fellow writers such as Willa Cather and Edith Wharton wrote to Fitzgerald to express their admiration for the novel. Indeed, poet T. S. Eliot had read it three times when he declared it "the first step American fiction has taken since Henry James" in a letter to the author dated December 31, 1925 (Eliot 2009, p. 813).

However, the novel failed to have the impact that Fitzgerald had hoped it would have and the disappointment was not easily—if ever—shaken.

A few weeks after publication, the Fitzgeralds were once again on the move, this time to Paris, where they rented an apartment at 14 rue de Tilsitt. Sometime toward the end of April, Fitzgerald finally met Ernest Hemingway, the writer whom he had praised to Max Perkins some months before. The only detailed record of this first encounter is in Hemingway's posthumously published memoir *A Moveable Feast* (1964). The accuracy of much of the book is deeply questionable with the depiction of Fitzgerald unflattering and cruel. The pair shared a close friendship for a while and Fitzgerald was crucial in Hemingway moving publishers to Scribner's. He was also instrumental in offering editorial advice to the younger man in relation to his first novel, *The Sun Also Rises* (1926). However, the relationship became increasingly strained and antagonistic as the years passed. Max Perkins, editor to both men, acted as an intermediary, communicating to both men about the other.

Over the next few years, the Fitzgeralds lived at different locations in Paris and the South of France as well as periodic returns to the United States. Both Fitzgeralds were drinking heavily but for Scott the tightening grip of alcoholism was interfering with his productivity. He was in increasing amounts of debt with both Scribner's and Harold Ober despite still being paid considerable sums of money for his short stories. For example, in 1926 according to Fitzgerald's own ledger his income was $25,686.05 (Bruccoli 2002, p. 532). Key events during this period were the beginning of a new novel shortly after the publication of *Gatsby* that would not see completion until 1934; publication of the important short story "The Rich Boy" (1926); a Broadway production of *The Great Gatsby* also in 1926; and a stint in Hollywood as a screenwriter in the opening months of 1927. The return to the United States during 1927 and 1928 also marked the beginning of Zelda's serious study of dance that would continue for a number of years with some success.

As the 1920s gave way to the 1930s a tidal wave of disaster struck both Fitzgeralds. The Wall Street crash of October 1929 drew to a close the carefree spirit of the Jazz Age with financial, psychological, and emotional ramifications for many. The unprecedented downturn meant a shrinking of the lucrative magazine market and the amount of money publications were prepared to pay for short stories, which directly affected Fitzgerald's livelihood. Compounding his growing financial worries and alcoholism, Zelda's mental health began to rapidly deteriorate leading to a complete breakdown that required hospitalization in April 1930. She would be in and out of expensive sanitoriums in Switzerland until September 1931 when the couple returned to the United States. In between, Fitzgerald had briefly returned to the United States in January of that year to bury his father. Zelda would go through the same upset when her own father, Judge Anthony Sayre, died in November 1931, marking a hellish eighteen months for the pair. The couple seemed to reflect on a personal level the distress and the chaos of the United States as the 1920s came to an abrupt halt and the Great Depression engulfed everything in its wake.

TENDER IS THE NIGHT AND "THE CRACK-UP" (1931–1937)

Fitzgerald had turned his attention to a new novel in the summer of 1925, mere weeks after the publication of *Gatsby*. More than five years later, the work remained unfinished. There were multiple drafts with multiple titles, a variety of plots that were amended and discarded, changes in focus and narrative voice during this period. Fitzgerald's inability to finish the novel was multifaceted. Financial anxiety weighed heavily upon him, which often led to him putting aside his novel to work on short stories that could pay the bills. Zelda's treatments and Scottie's education required a steady flow of income. Fitzgerald's alcoholism was also creating havoc in his personal and creative life as well as damaging his health and general well-being. He was also unable to get a handle on his material. This, in part, was because of constant interruptions, but there were possibly other factors too such as subject matter that was not best suited to his style and a dread of failure after the disappointment of the reception of *The Great Gatsby*.

However, early in 1932, he turned his attention once again to the novel and began to draft what would eventually become *Tender Is the Night* (1934). As a writer who drew heavily on his own life for inspiration in his fiction, Fitzgerald reflected upon recent events and funneled aspects of them into the novel. His growing familiarity with psychiatry because of Zelda's illness was a rich source of material and his protagonist, Dick Diver, is a psychiatrist who ends up marrying one of his patients. The novel is—in many respects—a reflection on the importance of work and vocation. It also reflects on the distractions that destroy the dedication required to succeed. Once again, it is possible to see Fitzgerald's themes reflecting concerns in his own life.

In February 1932, Zelda's mental health declined once again. It was serious enough to warrant admittance to Johns Hopkins Hospital's Phipps Psychiatric

Clinic in Baltimore. By the following month she had written a novel of her own titled, *Save Me the Waltz* (1932) and sent it to Max Perkins without any consultation with or mention of the work to Fitzgerald, who was mortified. Zelda had completed a full-length piece of fiction in six weeks compared to his six years of labor for no return. Even more unnerving was that the material crossed over significantly with his own novel with which he was starting to make progress. A bitter marital rift ensued with accusations of sabotage and demands to cease writing on Scott's part and claims of jealousy and stealing of her own experiences for his benefit on Zelda's. The relationship was becoming increasingly strained because of Zelda's ill health, Scott's alcoholism, and the relentless pressures the pair were under in their daily lives. Despite Fitzgerald's reservations, the novel was published by Scribner's on October 7, 1932.

By this time, Zelda had been discharged from the hospital and the couple were living at "La Paix." The house was on the estate of the Turnbull family and situated on the outskirts of Baltimore, Maryland. The Turnbull family's young son, Andrew, would be an early biographer of Fitzgerald's, publishing *F. Scott Fitzgerald: A Biography* in 1962. He also edited the first collection of the author's letters in 1963. During this time, Fitzgerald carried on working on his novel while Zelda turned her attention to writing a play called *Scandalabra*. It was produced by the Junior Vagabonds, a Baltimore-based theater group and had a one-week run in June 1933.

The final months of that year saw the beginning of Fitzgerald periodically checking himself into the hospital for a number of complaints. There were, of course, complications from alcohol but he also suffered from tuberculosis, the lung condition that had killed his beloved Keats.

By October, Fitzgerald was finally able to send Perkins the manuscript of his fourth novel, *Tender Is the Night*; the title came from Keats's poem "Ode to a Nightingale" (1819). The novel was serialized between January and April of 1934 in *Scribner's Magazine* and the book was finally published on April 12 of that year. It was an astonishing nine years since Fitzgerald had published a novel. Unfortunately, reviews were once again mixed. One of the perceived problems was that the novel's focus on a wealthy and leisurely class whiling away the days on the French Riviera seemed out of kilter with an America that remained in the throes of the Great Depression. To put this in context, *Tender Is the Night* was published less than three years before John Steinbeck's *Of Mice and Men* (1937) and only five before *The Grapes of Wrath* (1939). Both books detail the depths of the despair brought about by the economic collapse on great swaths of the American population. Other concerns were structural;

Fitzgerald had used an extended flashback in the middle section of the book, but some critics felt a chronological approach would have worked better. For others, there was also a sense of disjointedness because of the novel's lengthy composition and a feeling that Diver's demise was not fully explained. It is also worth noting that the anticipation after close to a decade of waiting almost guaranteed disappointment. Fitzgerald had his own reflections on the novel's perceived weaknesses when he wrote to Maxwell Perkins on March 11, 1935, almost a year after its publication:

> A short story can be written on a bottle, but for a novel you need the mental speed that enables you to keep the whole pattern in your head and ruthlessly sacrifice the sideshows as Ernest did in *A Farewell to Arms*. If a mind is slowed up ever so little it lives in the individual part of a book rather than in a book as a whole; memory is dulled. I would give anything if I hadn't had to write Part III of *Tender Is the Night* entirely on stimulant. If I had one more crack at it cold sober I believe it might have made a great difference. (Fitzgerald 1994, pp. 277–278)

Just before the release of *Tender Is the Night,* Zelda's mental health declined once more, and she was readmitted to the Phipps Clinic. She would be moved to a number of institutions over the next few years while her husband's circumstances became increasingly dire in terms of finances, productivity, and addiction. Between 1934 and 1936, he was moving between Baltimore and North Carolina, often in an attempt to be near where Zelda was hospitalized. In 1935, crippled by debt and worry and unable to work as quickly and effectively as in years past, Fitzgerald turned to his own inner turmoil as the source of a series of essays for *Esquire* magazine. After his death, they were published as a collection under the title of one of them: "The Crack-Up" (1945). The essays are powerful pieces of confessional writing in which the author reflects on the causes of his current plight and distress. However, Fitzgerald does play down the significance of alcohol as a root cause of his difficulties.

The series of essays were published in *Esquire* in 1936. It was a particularly painful year that saw his author friends berate him for exposing his emotional distress in a magazine. In addition, sometime friend and sometime nemesis, Ernest Hemingway openly mocked him by name in a story that was published in the same edition of *Esquire* that one of his own essays had appeared in. His mother died. He turned forty. On the day after his birthday that year, an interview was published in the *New York Post* that Fitzgerald had undertaken with journalist, Michael Mok. He was presented as a washed up, self-pitying drunk. Mortified and humiliated—according to a letter received by his long-suffering literary agent, Harold Ober, on October 5—Fitzgerald attempted suicide by overdose. Whether it was a genuine attempt or not, it clearly illustrated that the man was at the end of his tether.

HOLLYWOOD AND *THE LAST TYCOON* (1937–1940)

In the middle of 1937, Fitzgerald was given the opportunity to go to Hollywood to work as a screenwriter. He had done so twice before and—although not particularly enamored with either the work or the place—he grabbed the opportunity. Film studio MGM was prepared to pay him $1,000 a week on an initial six-month contract. Fitzgerald needed to address his debts and the movies offered a solution. By the time he headed west, he owed more than $22,000 (equivalent today to approximately $350,000–$400,000). An astonishing $12,511.69 was owed to Harold Ober alone (Bruccoli 2002, p. 419).

Although he spent the remainder of his life working in Hollywood and was assigned to a number of films during that period including *Gone with the Wind* (1939), Fitzgerald received only one screen credit for *Three Comrades* (1938) based on a novel by Erich Maria Remarque, best known for *All Quiet on the Western Front* (1929). However, the pay was good and despite intermittently falling off the wagon, Fitzgerald did maintain some level of sobriety allowing for a period of relative stability after the chaotic years of the early to mid-1930s.

Shortly after his arrival in Hollywood, Fitzgerald met English gossip columnist Sheilah Graham. They were romantically involved until the end of his life. Originating from London's East End, Graham had not been privy to an extensive education and Fitzgerald took it upon himself to be her teacher. He compiled reading lists for her, and she enthusiastically engaged with his mentorship, recounting the experience in her own book *College of One* (1967) written after Fitzgerald's death. The program of study revealed his own extensive reading. He also wrote regularly to Scottie, now at college, encouraging her to study and berating her when he felt she was not taking her work seriously. He valued education highly and wanted his own child to avoid the pitfalls that had tripped up her parents. Too often, Fitzgerald was—and still is—dismissed as a writer with a natural talent for lyricism but one that was not only undisciplined but unschooled in the literary traditions of which he was an inheritor. On close examination these seem unfair.

Fitzgerald may have formed a new relationship with Sheilah, but this did not mean that his commitment to Zelda disappeared. They remained in regular correspondence and he did not renege on his financial responsibilities toward her. They also spent some time together in North Carolina, Southern California, and Cuba. This final trip in April 1939, which was the last time the couple would see each other, involved Fitzgerald going on an alcoholic bender that required hospitalization on his return to the United States. The relationship as it once had been was over, but his commitment to her remained.

After a year and a half at MGM, Fitzgerald's contract was not renewed and he worked as a freelancer for a number of different studios including Paramount, Universal, and Twentieth Century Fox. His problems with alcohol recurred frequently much to the chagrin of Sheilah Graham. One particularly notorious episode occurred in February 1939 when he traveled to Dartmouth College to work on *Winter Carnival* (1939) with screenwriter Budd Schulberg. Fitzgerald was fired for drunkenness after being intoxicated nonstop for three days. Schulberg—who would go on to win an Oscar for best screenplay for *On the Waterfront* (1954)—recorded the events in his bittersweet novel *The Disenchanted* (1950).

This period of steady income had gone a long way to improve Fitzgerald's debts. In fact, he cleared money owed to Harold Ober completely. Unfortunately, the relationship would be terminated in July 1939 by Fitzgerald after almost twenty years when Ober—reluctant to return to the merry-go-round of debts and repayments—refused an advance requested by the author. Fitzgerald was deeply wounded and in an impulsive act, terminated their business arrangement and took to acting as his own agent, with little effect. However, Ober remained a surrogate father to Scottie, who had spent long periods of time living with his family. His role in her life is, perhaps, best illustrated by the fact that when she married—her father already dead—it was Harold Ober who gave her away.

Despite his work in the film studios, Fitzgerald never lost the sense that he was first and foremost a fiction writer. During this period, he began writing a sequence of stories about a Hollywood hack, Pat Hobby, who has fallen on hard times. There were seventeen stories in total and they were first published in *Esquire* magazine between January 1940 and May 1941. In the summer of 1939, he also turned his attention to a new novel set in the Hollywood studio system; it would be posthumously published as *The Last Tycoon* in 1941. He even hired a secretary to help him with this new project, Frances Kroll, who would recount the experience in her 1985 memoir, *Against the Current: How I*

Remember F. Scott Fitzgerald. Her death in 2015 at the age of ninety-nine severed Fitzgerald's last link with the living.

On December 21, 1940, at Sheilah Graham's apartment at 1443 Hayworth Avenue in Hollywood, F. Scott Fitzgerald died of a heart attack. He was forty-four. Two days after Christmas he was buried across the country in Maryland at the Rockville Union Cemetery. The Roman Catholic Church had refused permission for his remains to be buried in their cemetery nearby where his parents had been laid to rest. Zelda would join him in 1948 after being killed in a fire at the Highland Hospital where she was being treated for her ongoing mental health problems. In 1975, after the persistence of their only daughter was rewarded, the couple were reinterred in the Fitzgerald family plot at St. Mary's Church, Rockville, Maryland. Their headstone is inscribed with the closing line of Fitzgerald's most famous work, *The Great Gatsby:* "So we beat on, boats against the current, borne back ceaselessly into the past."

FURTHER READING

Bate, J. 2021b. *Bright Star, Green Light: The Beautiful Works and the Damned Lives of John Keats and F. Scott Fitzgerald.* London: William Collins.

Brown, D. S. 2017b. *Paradise Lost: A Life of F. Scott Fitzgerald.* Cambridge, MA: The Belknap Press of Harvard University Press.

Bruccoli, M. J. 2002b. *Some Sort of Epic Grandeur: The Life of F. Scott Fitzgerald,* 2nd rev. ed. Columbia: University of South Carolina Press.

Donaldson, S. 2012b. *F. Scott Fitzgerald: Fool for Love.* Minneapolis: University of Minnesota Press.

Tate, M. J. 1998b. *F. Scott Fitzgerald A–Z: The Essential Reference to His Life and Work.* New York: Checkmark Books.

FURTHER VIEWING

F. Scott Fitzgerald Society, www.fscottfitzgeraldsociety.org.

Niel, T., dir. *The Culture Show.* Season 2012–2013, episode 32, "Sincerely, F. Scott Fitzgerald." Aired May 18, 2013 on BBC (United Kingdom).

Prestwich, D., and N. Yorkin. *Z: The Beginning of Everything.* 2017. Santa Monica, CA: Amazon Studios.

Sage, D., dir. *American Masters.* Season 16, episode 2, "F. Scott Fitzgerald: Winter Dreams." Aired October 14, 2001, on PBS (United States).

Chapter 2
Literary and Cultural Context

When approaching a literary text—or any work of art for that matter—it is important to remember that it is not produced in a vacuum. The text reflects and engages with the social and cultural environment that it was created in. By having a greater understanding of these influences, the text becomes richer and understanding becomes deeper for the reader. What follows is an overview of some of the key historical and cultural contexts that were in play at the time that Fitzgerald was writing.

THE FIRST WORLD WAR AND ITS AFTERMATH

The impact of the First World War (1914–1918) extended beyond the battlefield and resulted in lasting cultural and social changes that were reflected in the art and literature produced in its devastating aftermath. Old Victorian certainties regarding the foundations on which society was built were revealed to be not so permanent after all. For example:

- Religious belief that suggested each individual life had value in the eyes of God was shown to be questionable when mechanized, industrial warfare permitted the extermination of tens of thousands of those lives in the course of a morning.

- Gender relations that confined women to the private sphere of the home seemed less "natural" in the wake of the mobilization of those same women on the home front because of the absence of their male counterparts.

- Class distinctions that affected every aspect of life in peacetime were blurred through the anonymity of uniform and the mixing of previously separated social groups.

- Similarly, widely held assumptions about race were also undermined (although not destroyed) in the face of military personnel being drawn from around the world and from every racial group.

The literature of this period and in the years after the armistice are deeply concerned with the permanent damage the war inflicted on the individual and social cohesion. In the midst of the fighting, poets such as Wilfred Owen shone a light on the generational division evident in the war, as young men were sent to the frontline to be injured and killed at the behest of older men far removed from the carnage. The questioning of established authority also destabilized national myths about the honor of dying for one's country, painfully explored in Owen's poem, "Dulce et Decorum est" among others.[1]

After the Armistice and through the course of the 1920s the war remained either the direct subject of European and American literature or a ghostly presence that haunts the novels, plays, and poetry of the period. Just as the conflict had left an indelible mark on the landscapes of France and Belgium, so it had permanently maimed its participants—both physically and mentally—in a way that had been previously unimaginable. In works such as Thomas Boyd's *Through the Wheat* (1923) and Ernest Hemingway's *A Farewell to Arms* (1929)

---

[1] The title of the poem comes from Roman poet, Horace. "Dulce et decorum est pro patria mori" (*Odes* III.2.13) translates as "It is sweet and fitting to die for one's country." Owen was killed on November 4, 1918, one week before the end of the war.

in the American context; and Ford Madox Ford's *Parade's End* (1924–1928) and Robert Graves's *Good-Bye to All That* (1929) in Britain, the horrific nature of the war is documented and explored. Alongside the explicit depictions of war, novels such as Hemingway's *The Sun Also Rises* (1926) and D. H. Lawrence's *Lady Chatterley's Lover* (1928) explore the far-reaching consequences of the conflict in terms of permanent physical injury, changing attitudes toward sex, female sexuality and emancipation, social mores, and class.

The significance of the war did not appear only in the work of those who had seen active service. Lawrence, for example, was rejected for military service because of his tuberculosis and marriage to a German woman. Despite Hemingway's numerous references to the conflict, he was an ambulance driver for the American Red Cross rather than a combatant, although he was seriously injured during a mortar attack. However, for participants and nonparticipants alike, this war was seen as the defining moment of a generation. For those who had seen action there was frequently a legacy of emotional and physical damage as well as an overwhelming sense of guilt that they had survived and hundreds of thousands had not. For those who had not participated, guilt and shame were accompanied by a sense of having been absent from the events that changed everything.

Fitzgerald was a commissioned lieutenant and he had undergone training; however, he did not take part in any military engagement, indeed he did not get overseas before the end of the war. Despite this the conflict can be traced in his work, most notably in the distinction he frequently makes in his novels and stories between those who had seen active service and those who had not. For example, the eponymous hero of *The Great Gatsby* (1925) and its narrator have seen active combat, but the military service of the novel's antagonist, Tom Buchanan, is not mentioned. Similarly (although with subtler significance), the main character in *Tender Is the Night* (1934), Dick Diver, did not have combat experience but his close friend, Abe North, did. Fitzgerald clearly understood the impact of both participatory and nonparticipatory experiences on character, attitude, and relationships both personal and social.

While focusing on the profound impact of this war on the generation of men born at the end of the nineteenth century as well as its social and cultural implications on the countries from which those men hail, it is worth noting that the American experience was different from that of their European counterparts in a number of ways. First, there is the shorter duration of the war for American combatants with U.S. entry occurring in April 1917. Second, and more important for our purposes, this conflict was not America's first experience of industrial warfare leading to an unimaginable number of deaths. The United States had seen such combat on its own land through the course of the Civil War (1861–1865) with the additional trauma of the self-inflicted nature of its wounds. The generation of Americans who saw (or did not see) action on the Western front were the sons and grandsons of men who had witnessed the horrors of the Civil War and its personal, political, social, and geographical aftermath. Fitzgerald and his two most significant white male contemporaries—Ernest Hemingway (1899–1961) and William Faulkner (1897–1962)—all had close family members who had been actively engaged in the Civil War and all three were highly knowledgeable about the conflict both in terms of family mythology and national history.

MODERNISM AND A CHANGING LITERARY LANDSCAPE

Even before the advent of the First World War, art and literature were going through a transformation of form in response to a changing world that was becoming increasingly industrialized and socially fragmented. Technological advancements such as photography and cinema had contributed to artists such as Henri Matisse (1869–1954) and Pablo Picasso's (1881–1973) experimentation with perspective, color, and the depiction of form. Picasso's Cubist movement that emerged in Paris in the teens and 1920s is considered one of the most influential art movements of the century. In poetry, American expatriate poet Ezra Pound (1885–1972) was rejecting Romanticism's traditional forms and experimenting with free verse that was rich in imagery, linguistic precision, and complex allusions. In 1914, he published an anthology of poetry—*Des Imagistes*—that included work by H.D. (Hilda Doolittle; 1886–1961), James Joyce (1882–1941), William Carlos Williams (1883–1963), Ford Madox Ford (1873–1939), and Pound himself.[2] Pound was also instrumental in the publication of T. S. Eliot's "The Love Song of J. Alfred Prufrock" in 1915.

In the 1920s these innovations coupled with the baffling and surreal horrors of World War I led to a series of key texts being published that would mark this decade as hugely significant in modernist literature. Influenced by Sigmund Freud's explorations of the human psyche, James Joyce's *Ulysses* (1922),

---

[2] At the time of publication Ford Madox Ford was known as Ford Madox Hueffer. He changed his name in response to World War I as he felt it sounded too Germanic.

continuing on from his 1916 novel *A Portrait of the Artist as a Young Man,* and *Mrs. Dalloway* (1925) by Virginia Woolf (1882–1941) experimented with narrative voice and the interiority of character. Through the technique of stream of consciousness, these writers—among others—attempted to mimic human thought as it is actually experienced. Artists of the period also rejected the notion of a single narrative, recognizing that all experience is unique to the individual rather than something that can be truly shared with others. The influence of Albert Einstein's Theory of Relativity can be seen in this departure from a belief in universal experiences. Narrative during this period becomes fragmented, distorted, and presented from multiple perspectives reflecting the collapse of faith in the old certainties of the prewar world. Other key texts of the decade are D. H. Lawrence's *Women in Love* (1920), *Point Counter Point* (1928) by Aldous Huxley, William Faulkner's *The Sound and the Fury* (1929), and the ongoing publication of Marcel Proust's *In Search of Lost Time* (1913–1927).

The artistic innovations that occurred at this time have had far-reaching influence on artists in the subsequent decades. However, the extent to which we can see Fitzgerald as a modernist writer, is far less clear. His lifelong love of the Romantic Poets ensured a particular approach to writing that embraced the lyricism that Pound, for example, rejected. That said, his first two novels did experiment with form to some extent. For example, the use of a script in *The Beautiful and Damned* (1922) instead of prose in one scene in the novel. However, these were largely unsuccessful. The novel that in many quarters is still the reason for his reputation, *The Great Gatsby,* cannot be seen as an experimental novel in the way that *The Sound and the Fury* can be. However, there are significant factors in this book that show Fitzgerald's engagement with the artistic movements around him even if their influence is more muted than in the work of some of his contemporaries.

Significantly, *The Great Gatsby* is set in the summer of 1922, the year that saw the publication of not only Joyce's *Ulysses* but T. S. Eliot's poem "The Waste Land." Fitzgerald was an admirer of both writers but importantly these two texts are seen as the two cornerstone texts of modernism. Fitzgerald's setting his novel in this year in particular can be seen as a nod to its literary significance. It could also be argued that Fitzgerald's major innovation in the novel is modernist in tone. His construction of the novel's first-person narrator, Nick Carraway, demonstrates an awareness of new approaches to storytelling, particularly in its rejection of one authoritative narrative as demonstrated in the nineteenth-century novel. Despite the novel not being deliberately obscure or difficult to read—as so often is the case with modernist texts—the potential unreliability of the character telling the story determines that the novel is open to multiple interpretations and responses. A brief survey of how Nick has been read by critics over the years is a telling indication of the complexities of *The Great Gatsby* that lurk underneath its readability.

THE ROARING TWENTIES

In the wake of the First World War and its monumental impact on social and cultural norms, the 1920s was a decade that broke free from many of the constraints of the previous Victorian and Edwardian world that had—in many respects—been blown to pieces on the Western front. There was a relaxation of the rigid social codes that had dictated the relationships between men and women as well as more interaction between classes and races. This, coupled with an explosion of popular culture in the forms of music, magazines, and cinema alongside growing consumerism and the advertising that accompanied it, created a period of energetic optimism.

A crucial contributing factor to the mood of the decade was Prohibition in the United States, which constitutionally outlawed the sale and manufacture of alcohol. The Temperance Movement had had a long history in the United States; its assertion was that social ills such as poverty, domestic violence, and premature death were linked to the consumption of alcohol. A ban on the sale of the root cause would therefore reduce the negative consequences with which it was associated. However, the unintended consequences of the law far outweighed the good (if any) that it achieved. Alcohol may not have been allowed to be sold legally but sold it was and in vast quantities. An enormous underground market was tapped into by organized crime that provided alcohol to speakeasies and illegal drinking establishments across the country with no regulation of the strength of the liquor being sold. Private individuals brewed their own batches of superstrength booze and Fitzgerald himself had a recipe for his own bootleg gin. Prohibition resulted in the birth of the American gangster (which Fitzgerald draws upon to create the murky background of Jay Gatsby and his money), an increase in violence, alcohol-related death, an uptake of drinking rather than an abandonment of it, and an astronomical loss in tax revenue that would have come through legal sales of alcohol.

The positive cultural impact of Prohibition was far reaching as it altered how and where people went for entertainment in cities like New York. There was an expansion of nightclubs where white patrons were exposed to the music of black Americans, most notably in the form of jazz. Fitzgerald would, of course, christen the period the Jazz Age and this music, with its roots in New Orleans, crossed over into the mainstream music of the time. Musicians such as Louis Armstrong (1901–1971) and Duke Ellington (1899–1974)—central figures of the Harlem Renaissance, which had seen a burst of black creativity in music, art, and literature in New York—would become household names.

The period would also be marked by a growing belief, conscious or otherwise, that associated success and happiness with material wealth. This attitude was spurred by an economic environment that encouraged conspicuous consumption to demonstrate economic power and therefore social influence. The tension between the promise of America at its inception—a place of individualism and self-realization—to its modern, early twentieth-century incarnation as a land that valued the dollar above all things in spite of its corrupting influence is a recurring theme in Fitzgerald's work.

The role of women was in a state of flux through the course of the decade. Women's right to vote in the United States was enshrined in law in 1920 and it marked an increasing independence from men. This liberation was simultaneously a source of excitement and anxiety for their male counterparts. Shifts in attitudes can be seen in changes in dress code and hairstyles through the course of the 1920s as both hemlines and hair lengths got shorter and the decade gave birth to the flapper. A mainstay of Fitzgerald's early fiction, the flapper was a young woman who flouted social conventions related to female behavior. She drank and she smoked, attended petting parties, wore more makeup than her forbears, and had the freedom of the automobile to get her from one party to another. As the culture of the chaperoned dance retreated, there was a relaxation of the codes of social interactions between the sexes that led to a more liberal attitude toward sex and relationships, which had its appeal for heterosexual men. However, it also represented a loss of masculine control over wives, girlfriends, and daughters resulting in an ambivalence toward women and female emancipation evident throughout Fitzgerald's work. He is simultaneously attracted to and repulsed by this new model of womanhood.

What is interesting about Fitzgerald's literary output during the course of the decade is, first, his perceptive documenting of contemporary life but second—and more poignantly—his awareness that it cannot last. Despite his enthusiastic engagement with the energy and excitement of a changing America, there is a melancholy undertone that indicates his awareness that a price has to be paid for the decade's excessiveness and its carefree approach to serious issues that bordered on reckless. There had to be a hangover from all that booze; there had to be a mountain of debt from all that spending. Fitzgerald was, of course, right both in a personal and a national context.

THE 1930S AND THE GREAT DEPRESSION

The economic environment of the 1920s was—like the decade itself—based on an unquestioning optimism. By the end of the decade, the stock markets were booming, and the prospect of an economic downturn seemed impossible. However, industry and agriculture were in overproduction and exceeding commercial demands, property prices were falling, consumer debt was growing to unsustainable levels because of cheap credit, and economic optimism had led to investors borrowing to buy stocks and shares. In addition, there was inadequate government regulation of banks, and many were small institutions that would not survive the economic strife that was approaching. The conditions for a perfect storm were in place.

On October 29, 1929, the trouble that had been brewing since September (when experienced investors began to question the values placed on shares and began to sell them) came to the fore in spectacular fashion. As investor confidence started to plummet there was a mass selling of stocks with sixteen million being sold on Black Tuesday. The stock market crashed and took the American economy with it. The impact would register far beyond U.S. shores triggering an economic downturn that was global.

Th effect on American life was immediate. Many investors were financially destroyed literally overnight; many banks folded as the panicked public withdrew deposits for fear of having their savings wiped out; unemployment, already on the increase before the crash, rose exponentially; and homelessness followed. It is estimated that as many as two million men became hobos during the early 1930s traveling around the country and living in tents and other makeshift accommodation. The problems faced by many were compounded by the fact that there was no social security system to support citizens who faced financial hardship and they were left to fend for themselves. Problems intensified further when a series of droughts struck the Midwest creating vast dust bowls that put even greater strain on an already struggling agricultural sector.

The mood of the nation was no longer enamored with the possibilities of American life; instead it was consumed with the need to simply survive it. There was considerable movement of people throughout the decade as the unemployed and destitute left one place to try and find work in another. In general, the move was westward as those caught up in the dust bowl that devastated the Midwest sought a new life. This, of course, caused its own problems as influxes of people threatened the job prospects of established communities causing further frustrations and resentment.

The difficulties and the desperation felt by the transient population was captured by photographers such as Dorothea Lange (1895–1965) and Walker Evans (1903–1975), who were charged with documenting the impact of the Great Depression by the Farm Security Administration during the second half of the decade. Many of the images captured by Lange and Evans are synonymous with the physical and psychological hardships of the 1930s on many Americans.

Alongside photographic documentation of the period, writers were also depicting these experiences in literature. John Steinbeck (1902–1968) in novels such as *Of Mice and Men* (1937) and *The Grapes of Wrath* (1939) explored in detail the plight of Americans who were forced to live lives that were transitory with little stability and no possibility of imagining—let alone planning—for the future. Erskine Caldwell in *Tobacco Road* (1932) depicted the fate of Southern cotton farmers who were at odds with the increasingly industrialized and urbanized world. His characters are trapped in poverty with few options, and through them Caldwell reveals the reality of a failing economic system.

Fitzgerald's only novel published in the decade had a very different tone from these realistic depictions of American life. *Tender Is the Night* (1934), set in large part on the French Riviera and other exotic European locations, was at odds with an American readership that were struggling to make ends meet. In perhaps—what is now—the most famous contemporary review, Philip Rahv writing in *The Daily Worker* closed his assessment of the novel with advice to the author stating "[d]ear Mr. Fitzgerald, you can't hide from a hurricane under a beach umbrella" (quoted in Bruccoli and Anderson 2003, p. 226). *The Daily Worker* was the mouthpiece of the American Communist Party, so it is unsurprising that Rahv had little time for Fitzgerald's cast of wealthy characters dissipating morally and psychologically through a lack of personal productivity. However, the reviewer did detect Fitzgerald's awareness that these characters are "[m]orally, spiritually, and even physically [. . .] dying in hospitals for the mentally diseased, in swanky Paris hotels and on the Riviera beaches" (225). The critic also unhappily detected that "Fitzgerald's eye discerns a certain grace even in their last contortions" (226).

However, much of Fitzgerald's work through the course of the 1930s was concerned with the difficulties of the decade. Admittedly, he did not focus on the characters that so preoccupied Steinbeck but he was in tune with the weariness felt by many. In stories, essays, and of course, letters, Fitzgerald pondered his own private Great Depression and attempted to find its causes and possible solutions. His series of essays for *Esquire* through the course of 1936, posthumously published as *The Crack-Up* (1945), explored his mental and financial collapse that resonated with the time. Earlier essays such as "Echoes of the Jazz Age" (1931) and "My Lost City" (1935) reflected on the contrast between the 1930s and the frivolous nature of the previous decade.

Similarly, his short stories took on a darker tone during the decade. "Babylon Revisited" (1931) is a study of a man trying—and failing—to escape the mistakes made during the dissolute 1920s. "One Trip Abroad" (1930), a precursor to *Tender Is the Night*, is concerned with the moral, spiritual, and physical decline of a married couple. In "An Alcoholic Case" (1937) Fitzgerald confronted through fiction what he was not prepared to fully acknowledge in life, namely the true, life-threatening nature of his alcoholism.

THE UNITED STATES VERSUS EUROPE

Fitzgerald, along with many of his American contemporaries, spent time in Europe and wrote about the experience of being an American abroad. It had been a rich feeding ground for earlier writers such as Henry James (1843–1916) who had explored the social and cultural tensions between the old and the new world. Fitzgerald was equally interested in the differences and tensions between the two. It could be argued that one of the questions posed by *The Great Gatsby* is how different from the old world is American society? Does the country really permit self-realization or does it demand conformity to imported hierarchies and social norms? In considering Fitzgerald's response to the European continent it is worth looking at it alongside the attitude to Europe of his fellow writer and sometime friend, Ernest Hemingway.

Hemingway spent lengthy periods in Europe (and beyond) but his engagement with his time overseas and his reasons for travel are markedly different from those of Fitzgerald, whom he would meet and befriend in Paris in 1925.

Hemingway originally arrived in the city in 1921 as a journalist for the *Toronto Star* with Europe as his patch. His journalistic writing was a key component in the development of his terse literary style, which has been imitated by many but arguably surpassed by none. However, his arrival in the city was seen by the young Hemingway as an opportunity to develop his fiction writing. These early years in Paris introduced him to a wealth of fellow writers, publishers, and artists who offered not only artistic advice but also career progression. Despite officially being in the city in the capacity of journalist, he had arrived with old-fashioned letters of introduction to key literary figures of the avant garde written by novelist Sherwood Anderson (1876–1941), whom he had befriended in Chicago. Letters were written to important figures such as translator Lewis Galantiere (1895–1977) and bookshop and lending library owner Sylvia Beach (1887–1962). Importantly, contact was also made with experimental poet Ezra Pound (1885–1972) and equally experimental writer Gertrude Stein (1874–1946) with whom Hemingway would enjoy close friendships. These older and more experienced artists acted as mentors to Hemingway as he honed his craft through their criticism.

Hemingway, and his wife Hadley, embraced the Parisian life, immersing themselves in the minutiae of the city. On their arrival they lived in a working-class neighborhood at 74 rue du Cardinal Lemoine near Place de la Contrescarpe. Despite Hemingway's later assertions of their poverty during this time, they had Hadley's trust fund to draw upon, and the myth of the struggling artist was somewhat exaggerated in typical Hemingway style. However, despite the frustration of trying to establish a career during this time, in later years the writer would cite this period as one of the happiest of his life. In his—not entirely reliable—posthumously published autobiographical work *A Moveable Feast* (1964), Hemingway recounts the early days of his writing career. In many ways his depiction of the writer absorbing Parisian culture, forming friendships, and developing his craft still haunts the popular understanding of the artist.

For Hemingway, Paris was an apprenticeship both in life and in art. It was the location that turned him from journalist (he gave up the profession in 1924) to novelist. In the years 1923 and 1924 he published in limited editions *Three Stories and Ten Poems* and *in our time*. In 1925, he would sign a contract with publishers Boni and Liveright and his first volume of short stories, *In Our Time*, would appear in October of that year. (This collection added additional stories to the previous collection of the same name.) Widespread success and notoriety would be achieved with the publication of *The Sun Also Rises* (1926), which drew heavily on autobiographical details of his life in Paris and his discovery of Spain during the early 1920s. By this time Hemingway had signed with New York publishing house Scribner's. This was in no small part because of the man that he met at the Dingo Bar in the spring of 1925: F. Scott Fitzgerald.

Fitzgerald's path to the City of Light was considerably different in terms of motivation to Hemingway's. The Fitzgeralds arrived in Europe for the second time in May 1924. They had made an earlier visit in 1921 that was not particularly successful. Fitzgerald had liked aspects of England describing Oxford as the most beautiful spot on earth. However, France and Italy did not fare so well. In a letter to Edmund Wilson he declared, "France made me sick" (Fitzgerald 1994, p. 47). So perhaps it is surprising that he headed once again to Europe a few years later. The motivation for Fitzgerald was not new experience, making connections, or developing his craft. It was for two reasons that run throughout his life story: money and productivity. After his early success with the publication of *This Side of Paradise* in 1920 and his generous renumeration for short stories for magazines such as *The Saturday Evening Post*, Fitzgerald was wealthy and famous. Swept along by the excitement of New York, success, and his wife Zelda, Fitzgerald had a tendency to spend money as soon—or even before—it was earned. His drinking was already problematic, and this, coupled with constant parties, resulted in a slowdown in his writing output. The change of scenery proved successful as Fitzgerald completed *The Great Gatsby* on the French Riviera before visiting Italy and then heading up to Paris in the spring of 1925. Fitzgerald rented a fully furnished apartment on the less avant garde Right Bank near to the Arc de Triomphe, removed from the working-class environs that Hemingway had initially embraced and the artistic center at Montparnasse to which Hemingway moved in 1924.

Shortly after their first meeting, Hemingway took Fitzgerald to meet Gertrude Stein at her salon: 27 rue de Fleurus. On their leaving Fitzgerald left a copy of *Gatsby*. Stein wrote to him shortly afterward to express her admiration: "We have read your book and it is a good book." She appreciated that he wrote "naturally in sentences and one can read all of them" (Wilson 1945, p. 308). An interesting comment for a high modernist writer to make. He was grateful for her appreciation but in contrast to Hemingway he had not sought Stein out nor had he made contact with Ezra Pound. During his time in Paris, he did know Sylvia Beach and he met on more than one occasion and greatly admired James Joyce, but the city did not seem to represent to Fitzgerald a place to engage in the exchange of intellectual or artistic ideas. This is often explained by suggesting that Fitzgerald was a talented writer in spite of himself. He was naturally gifted but lacking the necessary work ethic and intellectual engagement to be truly great. An idea perhaps best expressed by Hemingway, who wrote in *A Moveable Feast* that

> His talent was as natural as the pattern that was made by the dust on a butterfly's wings. At one time be understood it no more than the butterfly did and he did not know when it was brushed or marred. Later he became conscious of his damaged wings and of their construction and he learned to think and could not fly any more because the love of flight was gone and he could only remember when it had been effortless. (Hemingway 1994, p. 84)

However, this argument fails to acknowledge that Fitzgerald had read widely and was deeply entrenched in both the European and American literary traditions as well as being fully aware of the experimentation of the 1920s. Equally, the perfection of the structure of *Gatsby* and its exploration of America as an idea not a place hailed by many as *the* American novel belies the suggestion that he did not dedicate himself to his craft. His apprenticeship had, however, been overseen by his father's love of Byron and Keats and memories of the Lost Cause of the American South. Perhaps that ability to write "naturally in sentences," to quote Stein, in keeping with the Romanticism of his childhood and adolescence limited his interest in linguistic and artistic experimentation.

Fitzgerald's arms-length approach to artistic movements was mirrored in his attitude to the occupants of Paris too as he remained very much the tourist. He confessed to friend Edmund Wilson on his first trip to Europe that his observations of France might make him a philistine to which Wilson responded that Fitzgerald was "saturated" in America and its customs, its "hotels, plumbing, drugstores, aesthetic ideals and [the] vast commercial prosperity of the country—that you can't appreciate those institutions of France, for example, which are really superior to American ones . . . Settle down and learn French and apply a little French leisure and measure to that restless and jumpy nervous system" (quoted in Brown 2017, p. 120). Although Wilson's remarks are a criticism, there is a truth at the heart of them. Despite Fitzgerald's long periods in Europe, he remained a distinctly American author. Hemingway morphed and bled into the locations that he was living in and the place morphed and bled into his fiction, but Fitzgerald was different. His eye remained always American; he was never fully at ease outside of his homeland.

CHANGES IN HOLLYWOOD

Through the course of his career, Fitzgerald had three stints in Hollywood. The first was in January 1927 to write the script for a film called *Lipstick* that was never produced. There followed a brief period of only a matter of weeks in late 1931, and his final lengthy stay from the middle of 1937 to the end of his life in 1940.

Despite his dislike of Tinseltown, Hollywood played a significant role in Fitzgerald's life and career. It was a means of making money when his life and finances had hit rock bottom in 1936 and was the source material for a series of stories about a washed-up Hollywood writer, Pat Hobby, as well as the subject of his impressive if unfinished final project *The Last Tycoon* (1941). In many respects his dislike of this world is not surprising. The Hollywood studio system that he was working in drafted scripts collaboratively using teams of writers who could be moved at short notice to other projects. Even gaining a screen credit in recognition of their contribution to a film was not guaranteed. The system was therefore perhaps not a natural fit for a man who was used to working independently and being answerable to no one during the creative process.

Hollywood had changed considerably from its silent beginnings by the time Fitzgerald arrived for the final time in the late 1930s. The introduction of sound in 1927 with the film *The Jazz Singer* starring Al Jolson led to considerable changes in production, which now had to focus on more than just the moving image. How stories were told and who was telling them was also going through significant upheavals: "The studios had tended to hire ex-journalists or public relations agents for their contract writers, who did little more than construct serviceable plots. What dialogue they did write was severely limited to that printed on a few cards" (Fine 2013, p. 389). Unsurprisingly, the demand for experienced, professional writers increased with the advent of sound. Studios looked to the literary and theatrical circles of New York for talent that had been hit hard by the financial pressures of the Great Depression. Hollywood offered writers the chance to work for good money but artistic compromise was part of the deal.

The industry by this time was controlled by a handful of big studios: MGM, Paramount, RKO, Twentieth Century Fox, and Warner Brothers. There were also three smaller studios: Columbia, United Artists, and Universal. The advent of sound had led to mergers of companies into the five that dominated the industry. Hollywood had become very big business and had changed dramatically from the early days of small independent studios working with visionaries such as Charlie Chaplin and D. W. Griffith. These big corporations now controlled not only every aspect of production but also distribution and cinema exhibition. The industry was run by executives, rather than creative artists, who were more interested in turning a profit than in creative experimentation or innovation. What mattered was what sold. Many producers had little knowledge of the technicalities of filmmaking. However, they could control the story and through their relationships with writers influence the final product.

The industrial and collaborative nature of filmmaking also meant that it was a hugely expensive one. Many of the studios worked in the manner of a factory production line with most personnel, including actors, under contract and working exclusively for one studio with little say as to which projects they would be involved in. For writers, this meant scripts being moved along a string of writers who would polish dialogue or add humor or romance as required. For many writers the process was financially rewarding but soul destroying creatively. Some fared better by establishing relationships with a particular director, for example, William Faulkner's partnership with Howard Hawks. However, like Fitzgerald, Faulkner's time in Hollywood was financially motivated.

Undeniably, these final years were difficult for Fitzgerald. He was working in an industry he felt devalued his talents, Zelda remained unwell with no prospect of recovery, and he was apart from his daughter who was at college. However, he earned a decent wage that cleared his debts, he developed a relationship with Sheilah Graham, and he had periods of sobriety. Perhaps most important, he was working. As David Brown asserts, "[t]hough obviously a sick man during this period, he published over thirty stories and articles, worked on more than a dozen movie scripts, and wrote a publishable and promising *Tycoon*. Like Stahr [the hero of *Tycoon*], he kept his enterprise afloat, refusing to give way until he could do nothing else" (Brown 2017, pp. 326–27). It was in Hollywood that he would die on December 21, 1940 but he would leave Tinseltown behind and be laid to rest in his father's Maryland.

FURTHER READING

Berman, R. 2009. *Translating Modernism: Fitzgerald and Hemingway*. Tuscaloosa: The University of Alabama Press.

Curnutt, K., ed. 2004. *A Historical Guide to F. Scott Fitzgerald*. New York: Oxford University Press.

Curnutt, K. 2007. *The Cambridge Introduction to F. Scott Fitzgerald*. Cambridge: Cambridge University Press.

Latham, A. 1972. *Crazy Sundays: F. Scott Fitzgerald in Hollywood*. London: Secker & Warburg.

Mangum, B., ed. 2013. *F. Scott Fitzgerald in Context*. New York: Cambridge University Press.

Prigozy, R., ed. 2002. *The Cambridge Companion to F. Scott Fitzgerald*. Cambridge: Cambridge University Press.

Vaill, A. 1998. *Everybody Was So Young: Gerald and Sara Murphy: A Lost Generation Love Story*. London: Little, Brown and Company.

Chapter 3

Early Novels: *This Side of Paradise* (1920) and *The Beautiful and Damned* (1922)

I n many respects, the early novels—*This Side of Paradise* (1920) and *The Beautiful and Damned* (1922)—can be seen as Fitzgerald experimenting with and mastering his craft. Both books contain flaws in terms of structure that would be rectified when he reached artistic maturity with *The Great Gatsby*. Similarly, there is some attempt at experimentation that is not entirely successful but demonstrates an engagement with contemporary innovations in fiction that saw a breaking away from omniscient narrators and a single, accepted view of the fictional world. In terms of subject matter, he was more successfully in touch with the mood of the times; indeed, it could be argued that he was fundamental in creating it. He is particularly concerned in these novels with his generation and what made him and his contemporaries different from the generations that had come before in terms of social attitudes, life experience, and priorities. This focus on youth and—in *This Side of Paradise*—college life ensured that he garnered a wide readership, in particular, for his first novel.

Another key factor of his writing that would not be fully mastered until *Gatsby* is Fitzgerald's control of narrative voice. In both of these early novels, the narrator tends to be intrusive and overbearing with Fitzgerald almost offering a running commentary as to how the reader should respond to what is being read. As a result, the novels have a jarring quality that fails to fully immerse the reader as attention is constantly being drawn, in an unsophisticated manner, to their artifice. However, they remain important in charting Fitzgerald's progression as a writer in terms of style. They also are significant in their explorations of thematic concerns regarding marriage, vocation, alcohol, mental instability, and the impact of war, to which Fitzgerald would return repeatedly throughout the remainder of his career.

THIS SIDE OF PARADISE: COMPOSITION

As we saw in Chapter One, Fitzgerald's interest in writing had started early in life with short stories being written for school and university magazines as well as involvement with amateur dramatics as both writer and performer. However, when he turned his attention to writing a novel in the fall of 1917, after briefly flirting with the idea of poetry, he was attempting to leave behind his life as an amateur writer in the hope of turning professional. At the time that he began his first draft of the novel that would eventually become *This Side of Paradise*, he was still at Princeton. However, he had all but abandoned his college career and was waiting on an army commission after U.S. entry into the First World War. Perhaps a combination of wanting to justify his academic failure by undertaking a more significant project and the morbid preoccupation that he may, like many before him, die in a trench in northern France motivated him to literary action. Composition of this first draft, called *The Romantic Egotist*, was completed by March 1918 in the army camps that he was stationed in. It was rejected in August and then again in October of 1918 by Scribner's although there was evidence that Max Perkins, editor at the publishing house, was interested in seeing the novel in a redrafted format.

By the following year, Fitzgerald was in love with Zelda Sayre and keen to marry her. After he was discharged from the army, he headed to New York to work at an advertising agency while continuing with his writing. Zelda, unconvinced that Fitzgerald would make either career path a success, ended the engagement to a heartbroken Fitzgerald in June 1919. He retreated to his hometown of St. Paul with his manuscript to rewrite it once again. No doubt spurred on by the loss of Zelda and motivated by a wish to have a career that promised glamour as well as an income, Fitzgerald set to work. During a sustained period of work, he redrafted the novel from early July through to the end of August. He also changed the title to *The Education of a Personage* before settling on *This Side of Paradise*. The title was taken from the poem "Tiare Tahiti" (1915) by English poet Rupert Brooke.

In *The Making of This Side of Paradise* (1983) James L. West III, the leading textual scholar of Fitzgerald's work, traces the process of rewriting and revision undertaken by Fitzgerald during this time. He points out that a number of approaches that the author took to speed up the process of rewriting, and to keep in the book passages that he deemed worthy of preservation, contributed to some of the unevenness and implausibility of plot and mood. West points out that at the beginning of this period of redrafting, Fitzgerald was writing out everything in longhand. At times this involved copying word for word passages from *The Romantic Egotist* unchanged. At the beginning of this rewriting process Fitzgerald's methods benefited his work. West correctly asserts that:

> A typescript resists change; the determination to revise soon melts before the fixed verbal form and sequence on the paper. New thoughts must be made to fit between old ones, and a thoroughgoing revision is impossible. A fresh longhand draft, by contrast, takes its form as it goes. Its development is not hampered by an existing text. Even if the author is working with a previous version at his elbow, as Fitzgerald was doing here, he is free to expand, condense, add, delete—and to rethink. (West 1983, p. 46)

However, for whatever reason, Fitzgerald did not stick to the method that West notes significantly improved the first chapter. Possibly it was impatience to see the fruits of his labor that led him to turn to the cut-and-paste approach that he had initially resisted. West highlights the significant shortcomings of this on the novel as it shifts from being a redraft to a revision. The textual scholar, who has worked extensively with the manuscripts, asserts that this change in approach was detrimental to the construction of dialogue, sentence structure, and mood. New material was proving to be considerably better than what had appeared in the first draft of the novel. The impact of combining the new with old was an unevenness in quality and inexplicable shifts in the tone of some of the scenes. West writes that "[t]he old dialogue especially, was less effective than the new. Fitzgerald improved those old typescripts by revision and tinkering, but he was unable to refine out all of their weaknesses" (p. 47).

He continues by raising concerns about how scenes work alongside one another:

> When an author composes each scene in fresh holograph, he develops a sense, a "feel," for the ebb and flow of the work. His characters' moods and emotions must not shift abruptly without good reason; their attitudes must instead change gradually, and the reader must be prepared for these shifts. When an author is working with blocks of old typescript, however, he often finds it hard to recapture this feeling, and he is likely to juxtapose old scenes awkwardly. This is exactly what happened when Fitzgerald assembled Chapter Two. In a chillingly realistic section near the end of the chapter, Amory witnesses the bloody death of Dick Humbird in a car accident . . . Humbird had been an ideal of sorts for Amory, who is profoundly shocked by his sudden realization that human life is impermanent. But the very next night Amory is happily fox-trotting at the Spring Prom with Isabelle, having entirely forgotten Humbird's terrible death—or so we are expected to believe. (p. 47)

The final problem that West identifies with the redrafting of the novel relates to point of view. Fitzgerald—partly because his approach of mixing old material and new and partly because he did not have the artistic experience and maturity to master it—had incorporated the optimistic and somewhat naïve tone of his original first-person narrator to coexist with his third person omniscient narrator who has a world-weary and more cynical attitude. This creates an uneven tone that runs throughout the novel and is jarring and inconsistent.

Fitzgerald sent his revised book back to Max Perkins at Scribner's and on September 16, 1919, he received the letter that informed him *This Side of Paradise* would be published. The story of the novel, however, did not end there. As West has explored in great detail, the book on its publication was littered with spelling and grammatical errors that damaged Fitzgerald's reputation as a serious writer. Perkins did attempt to get these mistakes rectified in later printings, but the saga dragged on through a number of print runs. Despite these problems, the book sold exceptionally well and was not surpassed in terms of sales by any of Fitzgerald's novels in his lifetime. Between March 1920 and October 1921, the book sold approximately 49,000 copies (p. 111).

One hundred years after the novel's publication, *This Side of Paradise* does appear rather dated and self-conscious. However, within this novel are the beginnings of fiction that explores the experiences of teenagers and young people. The book is focused on how the lives and attitudes of the young are different from their parents and may indeed be quite shocking to them. It is possibly, therefore, not such a stretch to see in this book the seed that would grow into Holden Caulfield in J. D. Salinger's *The Catcher in the Rye* (1951) and the young adult fiction that subsequently emerged. The first step, perhaps, in the creation of the teenager that would be such a central figure in popular culture after World War II.

THIS SIDE OF PARADISE: SYNOPSIS

Amory Blaine is the child of a wealthy woman, Beatrice Blaine, who indulges her son throughout his childhood. She is the dominant force in his life and his father has minimal influence over him. Amory believes that he is exceptional and destined for greatness. He attends the St. Regis prep school where he is initially unpopular but eventually becomes the editor of the school paper and a football quarterback. Through his mother, he is introduced to Monsignor Thayer Darcy who will be pivotal in Amory's formation of his own sense of self.

After school, Amory attends Princeton but is more concerned with extracurricular activities such as the Triangle Club and involvement with the university paper, the *Princetonian*. During the Christmas vacation of his sophomore year, he falls in love with Isabelle Borgé. However, when she attends the prom at Princeton, the couple quarrel and break up.

During this period, Amory's father dies, and he realizes that the family wealth is dwindling. He also misses out on a number of opportunities at Princeton and fails important exams. Monsignor Darcy, with whom Amory is in touch, explains what he sees as the difference between what he considers a personality and a personage: "Personality is a physical matter almost entirely; it lowers the people it acts on—I've seen it vanish in a long sickness . . . Now a personage, on the other hand, gathers. He is never thought of apart from what he's done" (Fitzgerald 2012b, p. 101). Darcy asserts that both he and Amory are the latter. Amory meets and falls in love with his widowed cousin Clara Page, but she refuses to marry him. He graduates from Princeton and joins the army as the United States enters World War I.

During his time in the army (not detailed in the novel) his mother dies and he learns that his financial situation is worse than he had thought. He returns to America and takes an apartment in New York with two friends, Alec Connage and Thomas Parke D'Invilliers (who would reappear as the author of the epigram at the beginning of *The Great Gatsby*) as well as a job in advertising. He falls in love with Alec's sister, Rosalind, and the two discuss marriage. However, because of his financial situation Rosalind rejects him in favor of the wealthy Dawson Ryder. In response to this break up, Amory quits his job and goes on a three-week drunken spree.

After moving out of his apartment, Amory visits an uncle in Maryland. Here, he meets and falls in love with Eleanor Savage. She declares herself an atheist and refuses to conform to social expectations of womanhood. The relationship ends, however, when she threatens suicide by attempting to ride her horse over a cliff.

On a trip to Atlantic City Amory meets up with Alec Connage where he protects his old friend from accusations of sexual impropriety by pretending that it was he who was in a hotel room with a young woman, Jill Wayne. He learns that Rosalind is now engaged to Dawson Ryder; his inheritance has diminished further; and he is informed of the death of Monsignor Darcy. Weighed down by what he sees as the futility of life and disillusioned by the people around him, he attends Monsignor Darcy's funeral and heads back to Princeton. Amory has a discussion about socialism with the father of a young man, Jess Ferenby, with whom he had been at university and had been killed in the war. In the closing paragraphs of the novel and pining for Rosalind, Amory asserts that his generation was "dedicated more than the last to the fear of poverty and the worship of success; grown up to find all Gods dead, all wars fought, all faiths in men shaken . . ." The final line reflects the only certainty that Amory has: "I know myself," he cried, "but that is all—" (p. 260).

Fitzgerald was living in an age of rapid social change that included shifting attitudes toward the position of women in society on every level. There was a reconsideration of the nature of the relationships that women had with men as wives, daughters, mothers, and independent individuals. As a result, it is perhaps unsurprising that Fitzgerald reveals in the novel a simultaneous enthusiasm, anxiety, and ambivalence about both masculinity, femininity, and how the two interacted. His ambivalent response to womanhood can be traced through the course of the novel when the protagonist, Amory Blaine, encounters a series of women who represent "types" of female or aspects of the "feminine" that Fitzgerald had identified as both new and traditional forms of womanhood. He presents us with "the debutante," "the young widow," "the flapper," and "the free spirit." Motherhood is also represented in the form of Beatrice Blaine, a woman who is decidedly different from the author's own. These female characters reveal more about the ambivalence that Fitzgerald felt toward the changes that were occurring in America, particularly after World

War I, than they do about the reality of women and their lives during the period before, during, and after American involvement in World War I.

THE BEAUTIFUL AND DAMNED: COMPOSITION

The overnight success of *This Side of Paradise* published on March 26 and his marriage to Zelda Sayre on April 3 meant that the spring of 1920 was a time of excitement for Fitzgerald. The early weeks of the marriage were spent in hotels in New York drinking too much and throwing parties much to the unhappiness of hotel staff. They were young, beautiful, and famous. The lifestyle may have been enjoyable, but it was certainly not conducive to work. In May 1920, with the hope of a more regulated life, Fitzgerald rented a house in Westport, Connecticut. The location may have changed, but the lifestyle did not fundamentally alter. There were alcoholic parties that would last all weekend and beyond. Some of this drunken partying and the marital arguments that were one of its by-products were documented in the novel.

Fitzgerald drafted meticulous plans for what he hoped to achieve by the end of the year. It was a lifelong habit that did not always come to fruition. However, during the course of the summer, he wrote three stories: "The Jelly-Bean" published in *Metropolitan,* "The Lees of Happiness," which appeared in the *Chicago Tribune,* and "The I.O.U.," which did not sell (Bruccoli 2002, p. 143).[1] However, the novel was clearly on his mind; as Matthew Bruccoli notes, he wrote to Charles Scribner II—then president of Scribner's—in August 1920 summarizing the plot and thematic concerns (Fitzgerald 1994, p. 41).

The restlessness that marked much of the decade for the couple led them back to New York where they lived at 38 West 59th Street. Fitzgerald worked on the novel through the course of the fall and winter. By February 1921, Zelda was pregnant, and the couple decided to head to Europe before the baby arrived. Before their departure in May, Fitzgerald was able to send a draft of *The Beautiful and Damned* to his literary agent, Harold Ober, with the hope of selling it to a magazine for serialization. Ober sold the serial rights for $7,000.

They were not particularly enamored of their time in Europe. One highlight was Oxford in England that Fitzgerald deemed one of the most beautiful places

---

[1] "The I.O.U." was published in 2017 in a collection edited by Anne Margaret Daniel. *I'd Die for You and Other Lost Stories* contains stories that were not published in Fitzgerald's lifetime.

on earth. He also visited Cambridge and made a pilgrimage to Grantchester, where Rupert Brooke had lived at the Old Vicarage—the inspiration for one of his most famous poems. A second literary pilgrimage was taken to the Spanish Steps in Rome and the house where his hero, John Keats, had died of tuberculosis at the age of twenty-five. The couple also spent time in Paris.

By August, the Fitzgeralds were back in the United States living near St. Paul and awaiting the birth of their child. Fitzgerald spent time working on revisions of *The Beautiful and Damned* for its publication in book format. It was serialized in the *Metropolitan* between September 1920 and March 1921 but had been edited significantly by the publication rather than the author himself. The couple's daughter, Scottie, was born on October 26, 1921. On March 4, 1922, *The Beautiful and Damned* was published.

As is evident, the book was written in a frenetic period of the writer's life. He married, he became famous, he became wealthy, he became a father, he was on the move constantly, and at the time of the book's publication he was still only twenty-five. When considered in this light, Fitzgerald should be applauded for having finished the novel at all. However, the book does show the effects of an author not entirely focused on his craft. Just as in *This Side of Paradise*, Fitzgerald was not in control of his narrative voice and point of view. The novel is also episodic, which at times feels accidental rather than by design.

THE BEAUTIFUL AND DAMNED: SYNOPSIS

The Beautiful and Damned (1922) tells the story of Anthony Patch, heir to his rather puritanical grandfather's vast fortune, and his wife Gloria. The couple meet through Gloria's cousin and Anthony's friend Dick Caramel who is a novelist. Gloria is much admired by a number of men, including a filmmaker named Joseph Bloeckman who wants to marry her. However, Gloria chooses Anthony—despite the habit the two have of quarrelling—and dreams of the time when they will inherit his grandfather's money.

They take a house in Marietta in the countryside for the summer and spend the winter in Anthony's New York apartment. The relationship is at times tempestuous and Anthony's drinking increases. He attempts to write but with little productivity. His grandfather, Adam, arranges an opportunity for him to go overseas as a correspondent but he declines. Gloria is offered a screen test by Bloeckman but Anthony objects to it. The couple are living well beyond their means in part because of the shadow of Anthony's inheritance. However, Anthony does take a job—again due to his grandfather's influence—as a bond salesman. The couple and their friends Dick Caramel and Maury Noble go on a drunken spree to celebrate. The job, however, does not last long as Anthony quits and the couple ends up back in Marietta having renewed their lease at a drunken party.

Anthony's drinking continues despite Gloria's pleas to stop. During a drunken party, Adam Patch arrives unexpectedly and is appalled by what he witnesses and leaves in disgust. Anthony's attempts to reconcile with him are unsuccessful. With increasing financial woes, the couple move back to New York. Adam Patch falls ill and dies without reconciling with Anthony, who has been cut out of his will. Anthony retains a lawyer to contest it. The couple continue to squander money on weekly drunken parties. They lose a number of legal battles to overturn his grandfather's will.

America enters World War I and Anthony is drafted. He is deployed to an army camp in South Carolina where he has an affair with a local, working-class girl, Dot Raycroft. He maintains her as his mistress in a local boarding-house when he is moved to Mississippi. After the Armistice, Anthony is reunited with Gloria after having dissuaded her from traveling to the South during his deployment.

Reunited, the couple's marital and financial woes continue. Anthony takes a job and Gloria tries to get into the movies through their old friend Bloeckman. However, she is told by the film's director that at the grand old age of twenty-nine, she is too old for anything but a small, character role. Anthony quits his job and his drinking spirals out of control. The couple is forced to move to ever shrinking apartments and they are left close to penniless.

On the day that the last appeal is to be heard in court regarding the will of Adam Patch, Dot Raycroft appears on the couple's doorstep declaring her love for Anthony. He throws a chair at her and blacks out. Dick and Gloria tell him that he has won the case and is now in receipt of $30 million, but Anthony's mental health is evidently under strain when he tells them he will tell his grand-father if they don't leave.

Some months later, Gloria and Anthony are on a ship heading to Europe. Anthony is in a wheelchair and a couple observing him note that, "[h]e's been a little crazy, they say, ever since he got his money." They also mention that despite her good looks Gloria seems "dyed and *unclean*" (Fitzgerald 2008, p. 368). The closing lines of the novel reveal Anthony's thoughts about his life, his social position, and how he is perceived by others:

> Only a few months before, people had been urging him to give in, to submit to mediocrity, to go to work. But he had known that he was justified in his way of life—and had stuck it out staunchly. Why, the very friends who had been most unkind had come to respect him, to know he had been right all along . . .

> "I showed them," he was saying, "It was a hard fight, but I didn't give up and I came through!" (p. 369)

The novel is in many respects a reflection on the need for a vocation that is meaningful. The moral of the story of Anthony and Gloria Patch is that absence of such a focus in life results in dissipation and waste. In the final paragraphs, Anthony's inheritance may have now come to the couple, but Anthony is already broken. Despite Fitzgerald's depiction of Anthony's grandfather, Adam Patch, as a prig and a killjoy, he does seem to suggest that the old man has a valid point regarding what brings happiness and peace to a life.

The Beautiful and Damned is also concerned with the disappointment of married life after the excitement and anticipation of courtship. Once again, Fitzgerald explores the theme of the nature of desire and the paradoxical loss that is experienced when desire is fulfilled.

FURTHER READING

West, J. L. W., III. 1983. *The Making of* This Side of Paradise. Philadelphia: University of Pennsylvania Press.

FURTHER VIEWING

Curnutt, K. "Gatsby in Connecticut: *This Side of Paradise.*" Webinar from ATG Communications, April 3, 2020. https://vimeo.com/414282524.
Mastandrea, M., R. K. Tangedal, K. Curnutt, and R. S. Williams. "Gatsby in Connecticut: *The Beautiful and Damned.*" 2020 Pandemic Fitzgerald Webinar Series. Webinar from ATG Communications, June 5, 2020. https://vimeo.com/426773375.

Chapter 4
The Great Gatsby (1925)

In May 1940, Fitzgerald wrote to his editor at Scribner's, Max Perkins, in a desperate and despairing mood. Concerned that his professional reputation was all but eclipsed, he was keen to see his publisher keep *The Great Gatsby* in the public consciousness:

> Would the 25 cent press keep *Gatsby* in the public eye—or is it unpopular. Has it *had* its chance? Would a popular reissue in that series with a preface *not* by me but by one of its admirers—I can maybe pick one—make it a favorite with classrooms, profs, lovers of English prose—anybody. But to die, so completely and unjustly after having given so much. Even now there is little published in American fiction that doesn't bear my stamp—in a *small* way I was an original. (Fitzgerald 1994, p. 445)

His sadness and frustration are understandable; the royalties from his novels in the last year of his life were a paltry and ominous $13.13. Despite his work in Hollywood and his continued short story writing, Fitzgerald saw himself first and foremost as a novelist. His melancholy reflections in this letter indicate that he realized with bitterness that the world did not.

After his death, he did—of course—reemerge from the shadows, first, with the posthumous publication of *The Last Tycoon* (1941) under the editorship of his old friend, Edmund Wilson. Second—and perhaps more important for his resurrection as a novelist—in 1945, *The Great Gatsby* was reissued by the Editions for the Armed Services, opening up his work to a new generation of readers when the book was given to service personnel at home and abroad. The Second World War, therefore, played a role in fulfilling the wish Fitzgerald had so dearly hoped for in his letters to Perkins. Through the course of the 1950s and 1960s Fitzgerald attracted increasing scholarly and biographical attention. The cornerstone of Fitzgerald's studies was *Gatsby* from the very beginning, and this remains the case despite growing interest in other aspects of his work. The book has now sold in excess of twenty-five million copies, with annual sales of 500,000 according to Scribner's. The book has come a long way—both in terms of popularity and critical success—from the day of

Fitzgerald's death when Scribner's still had copies of the novel from its second print run from 1925 gathering dust in its warehouse. Fitzgerald's second wish in that forlorn letter to Perkins has also come to pass as *The Great Gatsby* is indeed "a favorite with classrooms, profs, lovers of English prose." If only he had lived to see it.

COMPOSITION

In April 1924, Fitzgerald turned his attention to the writing of his next book. Since the publication of *The Beautiful and Damned* (1922), he had been fitfully working on a novel but with little success. As early as June 1922, he communicated to Perkins that he was considering a number of ideas concerning location, period, and the timescale of the narrative events. "Its locale will be the middle west and New York of 1885 I think." He also indicated that "[i]t will concern less superlative beauties than I run to usually + will be centered on a smaller period of time" (Fitzgerald 1994, p. 60). However, in the spring of 1924 he wrote to Perkins once again about his plans for the novel:

> Much of what I wrote last Summer was good but it was so interrupted that it was ragged + in approaching it from a new angle I've had to discard a lot of it—in one case 18,000 words (part of which will appear in the Mercury as a short story). It is only in the last four months that I've realized how much I've—well, almost *deteriorated* in the three years since I finished the Beautiful and Damned. (p. 67)

The story that was salvaged from the discarded material was "Absolution" published in June 1924. The links between the story and *The Great Gatsby* have garnered plenty of scholarly attention and it is very much seen as a precursor to the novel. Along with this material, Fitzgerald also scrapped the idea of setting his story in 1885; instead he turned his attention to contemporary America.

Having found a new resolve to get the novel completed and shored up by lucrative short story writing, Fitzgerald headed to Europe in the spring of 1924 to work. The exchange rate also buoyed up his finances, permitting an uninterrupted period of creativity through the summer and fall. The novel was sent to Perkins in October 1924.

What is evident throughout the letters of this period is Fitzgerald's commitment to creating a perfectly structured, economical, and controlled piece of literature. Anything that does not contribute to the development of character or plot is removed; there are no inconsequential scenes, dialogue, or characters. Letters exchanged between Fitzgerald and Perkins from October 1924 to the novel's publication on April 10, 1925, show a huge amount of attention paid to redrafting and editorship in order to achieve the vision that Fitzgerald had for the work. There is a willingness to take on board advice given by Perkins to improve the text. Most notably Perkins suggested that more detail should be given about Gatsby's background and appearance. This led to Fitzgerald's masterful description of his protagonist's smile that reveals as much about his character as it does about his physicality. On other points, Fitzgerald was adamant that changes should not be made; for example, the brutal image of Myrtle's breast ripped from her body at the time of her death. It would seem nothing would stop Fitzgerald from achieving his goal of creating "something *new*— something extraordinary and beautiful and simple and intricately patterned" (Bruccoli and Baughman 2004, p. 17).

SYNOPSIS

The events of *The Great Gatsby* are told in the first person by narrator Nick Carraway, a Midwesterner and World War One veteran, who moves to New York in the spring of 1922 to work as a bond salesman on Wall Street. Although the move is supposed to be permanent, Carraway's experience during the summer months have shaken and repulsed him to such a degree that he returns to his hometown in the fall and it is from there that he is telling the story of those events.

On arriving in New York from the Midwest the previous year, Nick decides not to live in the city and instead he finds a bungalow for $80 a month amid the new money and mansions of West Egg, Long Island. Next door lives a man called Gatsby but that is all Nick knows about him. Across the bay—in the more fashionable East Egg—Nick's distant cousin Daisy lives with her incredibly wealthy husband Tom Buchanan who was a contemporary of Nick's at Yale. The events of the novel begin when Nick visits the couple for dinner. While there, he is introduced to Jordan Baker, an amateur golfer and close friend of Daisy. She will reveal to Nick through the course of the evening that she is familiar with his neighbor, Mr. Gatsby, and that Tom is having an affair with a woman in

New York. Nick and Jordan will later embark on a love affair. After dinner, Nick returns home and catches sight of Gatsby on his expanse of lawn stretching his arms out to a green light on the other side of the bay.

Nick is introduced to Tom's mistress, Myrtle Wilson, who lives with her husband George above the garage that he runs in the "valley of ashes." It is an industrial wasteland and dumping ground halfway between New York and Long Island. Tom has rented an apartment for Myrtle in the city where they conduct their affair. During a drunken party that Nick attends, an argument between Tom and Myrtle over Daisy erupts and ends when Tom brutally breaks his mistress's nose.

During the course of the summer, parties are frequently held at Gatsby's mansion with music and alcohol aplenty. Early one Saturday morning a chauffeur arrives at Nick's with an invitation to attend Gatsby's next party that evening. Nick arrives at Gatsby's mansion and is convinced that he is one of the few people present who has actually received an invitation. Instead, people gravitated to Gatsby's house from the city having little idea who their host is or even what he looks like. Nick bumps into Jordan and the two spend most of the evening together. A man starts up a conversation with Nick, recognizing him from time spent overseas during the war and much to Nick's embarrassment, he is revealed to be Gatsby himself. Later in the evening, Gatsby asks to speak to Jordan privately.

One morning toward the end of July, Gatsby arrives at Nick's to take him to lunch in New York. On their drive into town, Gatsby recounts his wartime experiences and his history, aspects of which Nick finds fantastical. Gatsby also tells Nick that he has asked Jordan to make a request of Nick when the pair meet up that afternoon, much to Nick's annoyance. During lunch they meet one of Gatsby's murky business acquaintances, Meyer Wolfshiem, as well as bumping unexpectedly into Tom. After Nick exchanges a few words with him he turns around to find Gatsby gone.

When Nick meets Jordan later the same day, she tells him that Gatsby had known and loved Daisy before she married Tom. They had met in 1917 when he was in the army and stationed at Fort Taylor near her home in Louisville, Kentucky. After Gatsby was sent overseas and did not immediately return after the armistice, Daisy became involved with Tom and agreed to marry him. She also reveals that Tom's infidelity with Myrtle is not his first and such betrayals started at almost the very beginning of their marriage. Jordan tells Nick that Gatsby had chosen his house because it was across the bay from where Daisy lives and that he had thrown all those parties in the hope that she would appear at one of them but to no avail. Gatsby asked Jordan if she would ask Nick if he would ask Daisy to tea so that he can be reunited with her. On his return home he sees Gatsby and he agrees to make arrangements for Daisy to come over. A few days later Gatsby and Daisy are reunited at Nick's and their affair is rekindled.

Over the next few weeks, the affair intensifies, and Tom starts to become suspicious of Daisy's frequent absences. On one Saturday night the Buchanans attend one of Gatsby's parties. Daisy is rather taken aback at what she perceives to be the vulgarity of the place, and Tom's interest in finding out more about Gatsby and his background increases. After this, the parties that had been the mainstay of the summer come to an abrupt halt.

Nick and Jordan are invited to lunch at Tom and Daisy's with Gatsby. The lovers have decided to tell Tom about their relationship and call on their friends to be there. As the tension mounts—only increased by the oppressive heat—Daisy suggests they drive into town. When Tom suddenly recognizes the true nature of the relationship between his wife and Gatsby without them saying a word, he agrees. The party travels in two cars with Tom driving Nick and Jordan in Gatsby's car and Daisy and Gatsby travelling in Tom's car. Tom stops at Wilson's garage and finds out from Myrtle's husband he intends to move West with his wife and implies that he has discovered she is having an affair.

In New York, they rent a suite at the Plaza Hotel and a confrontation between Tom and Gatsby takes place. Tom exposes his rival as a bootlegger with murky business connections. Daisy's retreat is almost immediate. The party breaks up and they head home with Daisy traveling with Gatsby in his own car. Tom, Jordan, and Nick follow. However, as they pass through the valley of ashes they stop to find that Myrtle has been killed by a car that matches the description of Gatsby's.

On their return to East Egg, Nick refuses to go into the Buchanan house and rejects Jordan. He discovers Gatsby hiding by the Buchanan residence to make sure Daisy is okay. Gatsby then reveals it was Daisy who was driving the car but that he would take responsibility for Myrtle's death. The next morning back at Gatsby's house, he reveals to Nick the reality of his past. He came from a poor farming family in South Dakota and he realized that his meeting with Daisy was possible only because of the anonymity of his uniform. He had gone on to make his money by whatever means necessary in the hope of winning her back.

Meanwhile, Tom tells George that it was Gatsby who had killed Myrtle and had been having an affair with her. Heartbroken and filled with rage Wilson heads out to the West Egg mansion where Gatsby is waiting in his swimming pool for a telephone call from Daisy that never comes. George shoots him dead before turning the gun on himself.

Nick arranges the funeral but no one other than Gatsby's father and one of the regular guests at his parties attends. Nick is horrified that Daisy does not even send a message. He is equally disgusted that none of the many people who had taken advantage of Gatsby's hospitality came to show their last respects as they tried to distance themselves from the growing scandal.

Nick makes a final break with Jordan. He also bumps into Tom who tries to justify his actions but Nick is repulsed by what he has seen and been a part of during the summer months. In disgust he packs his belongings and heads back to the Midwest, forever changed by events but still enamored with Gatsby's "extraordinary gift for hope" that is encapsulated in the final sentences of the story that he tells.

THEMES

The Great Gatsby is a novel just short of 50,000 words. Despite its brevity, it explores a range of themes that go beyond the idea of the American Dream with which it has so often been associated. The approach taken here is to explore the themes of the novel through its motifs, characters, and structure. However, key themes of the novel are self-realization, modern life, love, disillusionment, and the nature of desire, but perhaps most important, the novel is about America and not just its much-vaunted dream. Fitzgerald is concerned with what America is, what it was supposed to be, and what it can be. He identified his country's uniqueness in his short story "The Swimmers" (1929), and it is this that is his greatest theme not only in *The Great Gatsby* but throughout the very best of his work:

> France was a land, England was a people, but America, having about it still that quality of the idea, was harder to utter—it was the graves at Shiloh and the tired, drawn, nervous faces of its great men, and the country boys dying in the Argonne for a phrase that was empty before their bodies withered. It was a willingness of the heart. (Fitzgerald 1989, p. 512)

His complex depiction of the country in the novel suggests disappointment in its failure to live up to the ideals on which it was founded. In this regard Fitzgerald is particularly focused on the concept of America being a land that permitted its citizens to reinvent themselves. Gatsby and Myrtle attempt to escape the life into which they were born but do not succeed in this quest, in part because of the failure of American society to permit such a change. This pessimism is tempered by a hope that America will fulfill its promise in time, but in the closing lines of the novel, the suggestion is that it is a pursuit that may never come to an end. Nick reflects on Gatsby's belief in the green light but then shifts from the focus on one man to include us all. Just as the green light eluded Gatsby, "[it] eluded us then, but that's no matter—tomorrow we will run faster, stretch out our arms farther. . . . And one fine morning—" (Fitzgerald 2019, p. 218).

STRUCTURE

One of the most significant departures Fitzgerald made in *The Great Gatsby* in comparison to his two earlier novels is the attention he paid to the novel's structure. It consists of nine chapters, fairly even in length. The focus of each is a social gathering or party of some description. Chapter One shows the dinner party at the Buchanans, followed by Chapter Two's depiction of the party at Myrtle's New York apartment. Chapter Three is the introduction to Gatsby's grand, elaborate parties and Chapter Four shows the lunch between Gatsby, Nick, and Meyer Wolfshiem when they bump into Tom. Chapter Five, which is the center point of the book, depicts the reunification of Gatsby and Daisy. Chapter Six is focused on the party at Gatsby's attended by the Buchanans and the following chapter is the disastrous gathering at the Plaza Hotel. Chapter Eight sees Nick spend the early hours of the morning after Myrtle's death with Gatsby and breakfast with him before telling him that "[t]hey're a rotten crowd . . . [y]ou're worth the whole damn punch out together" (Fitzgerald 1994, p. 185). The final chapter includes the sorrowful depiction of Gatsby's funeral.

The story is told retrospectively so it is important to be aware that Nick—as he is narrating the story—already knows its outcome. By keeping this in mind, it is possible to identify contradictions in his narrative. It also reveals Nick's conflicting responses to situations as they occurred and his responses to those same events as he looks back on the story. It is in Fitzgerald's construction of the novel's narrative voice that the profound complexities and ambiguities of the text can be located.

Although the novel gives the impression of occurring in chronological order with one narrator there are disruptions in both aspects of the novel. For example, Fitzgerald introduces Gatsby's backstory in Chapter Six although chronologically it is told much later, in Chapter Eight. Indeed, Gatsby tells Nick of his past on the morning that he is killed. In terms of narration Nick gives way to Jordan who narrates the first meeting between Gatsby and Daisy in the first person. The seamlessness of Nick's narration throughout the novel also means that it can go unnoticed that Nick recounts the events of the aftermath of Myrtle's death with a level of detail and dialogue that goes far beyond hearing the story second hand. However, the suspension of the reader's disbelief is unaffected by this or by Nick's repeated intrusions into the mind and emotions of Gatsby. Throughout the novel, Nick knows things—or asserts that he does—that he could not possibly know.

A final structural device used by Fitzgerald in the course of the novel is the use of a variety of methods to convey information. He includes references to "reliable" sources such as newspapers and coroner's reports but also includes unreliable sources of information such as gossip and partially overheard conversations. Gatsby's youthful schedule of improvement is written in the back of his childhood copy of *Hopalong Cassidy*. Nick's list of Gatsby's guests written on the back of a train timetable includes information about the fate of some of the people he crossed paths with in Gatsby's moonlit garden. There is Meyer Wolfshiem's letter to Nick in the aftermath of Gatsby's death distancing himself from the man and the events—a rather old-fashioned form of communication when coupled with the telephone calls that play an important role in the plot. Finally, there are extensive references to popular culture and music throughout the course of the novel.

MOTIFS

Through the course of the novel, Fitzgerald uses a series of motifs to represent its central themes and to create mood. Some of the images provide *The Great Gatsby* with its haunting quality. The green light, Gatsby's blue gardens, and the yellow cocktail music that fills them are difficult to forget. Some of the motifs, however, are closely aligned with the text's thematic concerns such as American identity and modernity.

The Green Light

The most famous symbol in the whole of the novel, possibly in all of American literature, is the green light at the end of Daisy's dock, "minute and far away" that Gatsby stretches his arms toward at the end of the first chapter of the novel (Fitzgerald 2019, p. 26). Fitzgerald's decision to embody Gatsby's dreams and desires in a physical object paradoxically adds to the intangible quality of them as it allows the author to refuse a full articulation of them. He preserves throughout the novel "the elusive rhythm, a fragment of lost words" that Nick "almost remembered [but] was uncommunicable forever" (p. 134). It is the enigma that lies at the heart of the novel.

Of course, despite its unfathomable quality, there have been repeated attempts to explain the significance of the green light. One interpretation—and the simplest—is that it is representative of Daisy. It is a literal symbol that indicates to Gatsby the nearness of both the woman he loves and the realization of his dream. However, this interpretation begins to buckle under the weight of Nick's reflections when the couple are reunited. After Gatsby points out to Daisy the green light, Nick observes "[p]ossibly it had occurred to him that the colossal significance of that light had now vanished forever . . . [h]is count of enchanted objects had diminished by one" (pp. 112–113). What Nick perceives here is that Gatsby is mistaken about the significance of the green light. He is wrong to believe it represented Daisy, as Daisy is shown to be—not the object of his pursuit—but another symbol of his "unutterable" dream. Nick's melancholic reflections on seeing the "faint doubt" in Gatsby's face sums up Gatsby's misapprehension: "There must have been moments even that afternoon when Daisy tumbled short of his dreams—not through her own fault, but because of the colossal vitality of his illusion" (p. 116).

A second interpretation is that it is symbolic of the American Dream, a term that was popularized by James Truslow Adams in *The Epic of America* (1931). It is worth noting this volume was published six years after *Gatsby*; however, the concept is one that has run through American society since its inception by European settlers. This is a place that allows the individual to strive to reach their potential, to make dreams a reality no longer hindered by hierarchical structures of the Old World that trapped men and women to limited lives because of the accident of their birth. It is a land of possibility; it is a land of self-invention. This interpretation works reasonably well until we consider Gatsby's fate at the end of the novel. He is destroyed by his social and romantic presumptions and breaks apart when he comes face to face with "Tom's hard malice" (p. 177). Jimmy Gatz's attempts at reinvention are destroyed by a society, represented by Tom Buchanan, that under examination is not so very different from the European one that it had supposedly left behind.

The green light could represent self-realization that is not bound by societal expectations that equate success with money, social influence, and artificial hierarchies. It could be the individual pursuing his or her vocation with little regard for the opinion of others in creating a sense of self that brings genuine fulfillment. It is this that Gatsby surrenders when he amalgamated his dream of self-realization with the social acceptance that comes from marriage to the famed golden girl and explains Gatsby's "faint doubt" at the couple's reunion (p. 116), a compromise that has left the green light forever unobtainable to him. This interpretation is of particular interest when looking at an earlier version of the novel under the title *Trimalchio*. In the scene that would become the famous "can't repeat the past" scene in the published novel, Nick points out that Daisy is "a person" not just "a figure in your dream" and "probably doesn't feel that she owes you anything at all."

Gatsby's response is immediate: "'She does though. Why—I'm only thirty-two. I might be a great man if I could forget that once I love Daisy. But my career has to be like this—' He drew a slanting line from the lawn to the stars. 'It's got to keep going up. I used to think wonderful things were going to happen to me, before I met her. And I knew it was a great mistake for a man like me to fall in love—and then one night I let myself go, and it was too late . . .'" (Fitzgerald 2000, p. 90).

Whatever it represents for the reader of the novel, one thing is clear. The green light is a reminder that so often in life, the pursuit of the dream is more exciting and satisfying than the achieving of it. The green light is the desire for something or someone. Once it is achieved the desire is destroyed and the reality is invariably a disappointment. It is in this presentation of desire and loss that the profound nostalgia evident in much of Fitzgerald's work is rooted. Perhaps the green light should always be "minute and far away" (Fitzgerald 2019, p. 26).

West Egg versus East Egg

In Fitzgerald's fictionalized geography of East and West Egg, the author is able to explore some of the novel's major thematic concerns by contrasting the people that inhabit each place. Nick introduces the two Eggs as "one of the strangest communities in North America" and subsequently states the noteworthiness of "their dissimilarity in every particular except shape and size." West Egg is the less fashionable of the two and, rather intriguingly, Nick continues his description by saying that "this is a most superficial tag to express the bizarre and not a little sinister contrast between them." In essence, the two are separated along the lines of old and new money.

This is effectively conveyed with the brief descriptions given of Gatsby's mansion and the home of the Buchanans. The former is described as "a colossal affair by any standard—it was a factual imitation of some Hôtel de Ville in Normandy, with a tower on one side, spanking new under a thin beard of raw ivy, and a marble swimming pool, and more than forty acres of lawn and garden" (pp. 5–6). The mansion is the same as its occupant; new wealth attempting and failing to disguise itself as something old and established. In contrast, Tom and Daisy live in "a cheerful red-and-white Georgian Colonial mansion, overlooking the bay" (p. 8). It is authentic. Fitzgerald's personification of the house and its lawn creates the sense that it has evolved over time and belongs to this place, a natural product of its environment. In contrast the factual description of Gatsby's house, almost as a checklist of necessary features, feels forced and artificial.

Fitzgerald highlights the differences in the occupants of East and West Egg when Nick observes the languid, relaxed, and inconsequential conversation of Daisy and Jordan and contrasts it with the eager and anxious activity of West Eggers. These women "knew that presently dinner would be over and a little later the evening would be over too and casually put away." Nick notes this is completely opposite to the unease and discomfort found in Gatsby's neck of the woods "where an evening was hurried from phase to phase toward its close, in a continually disappointed anticipation or else in sheer nervous dread of the moment itself" (p. 15).

In broader terms, the notion of East and West Egg can be extended to the whole of the nation. The American West has often been seen as a place of pioneers, new beginnings, and the individual fulfilling their own dreams and ambitions. It is wild and untamed. The East, in contrast, is associated with social order, civilization, and European values. This contrast in the geographical regions of the country is the basis of that most American of genres, the Western, in which geography is used to explore the nature of the American spirit. Fitzgerald draws upon the dichotomy of East and West to explore—if not answer— this question too.

The Valley of Ashes

The bleak valley of ashes situated between the glamorous settings of New York City and Long Island, provide a stark contrast to them. However, the necessity of passing through the valley to get to either location means it is also a reminder for the reader and the characters—if they took the trouble to notice—that underneath the glamour and excitement of modern America there is a desperate underbelly.

Fitzgerald's depiction of the valley is deeply influenced by T. S. Eliot's "The Waste Land" published in 1922, the year the novel is set. In Eliot's groundbreaking poem, he explores the fragmented and fractured nature of modern life with its cacophony of voices, the despair evident in city life, and disillusionment. Fitzgerald depicts a similarly hopeless environment that is overseen not by the eyes of God as in previous centuries but by an advertising billboard for Dr. T. J. Eckleburg. Commerce and money have replaced an omniscient being as the object of American worship, just as the omniscient narrator has been replaced by an unreliable one in modern literature.

It is to the enormous eyes of Eckleburg that George Wilson will appeal, even if he "[d]on't belong to any" church, after the death of Myrtle Wilson (p. 189). His despairing cry of "God sees everything" may seem to be the expression of the anger and sadness of a man in desperate need of an explanation as to why this has happened to him. However, in some respects he is correct, the reader—overseeing the world of the novel—may not have seen everything, but it has been revealed to them. The misery and unhappiness of men like George, the yearning for a better life in women like Myrtle, the dreams of Gatsby have been seen by the reader. The brutal, careless treatment of them by men and women like Tom and Daisy has also been exposed through the course of the text. However, in a godless age, punishment does not appear to follow.

The Automobile

Fitzgerald, throughout the course of the novel, uses the car as a symbol of modern American life. It suggests the newfound freedoms for both men and women as well as a growing interconnectivity across the nation. Fitzgerald, however, also uses it as a motif to represent the recklessness found in American society during the course of the decade. In 1924, the year before *The Great Gatsby* was published, an astonishing 23,600 deaths occurred on the nation's roads, alongside 700,000 injuries and property damage totaling more than $1 billion.[1] Fitzgerald uses the bloodshed on the nation's roads not only as

---

[1] Statistics were obtained from http://www.autolife.umd.umich.edu/Environment/E_Casestudy/E_casestudy7.htm Accessed December 9, 2020.

inspiration for the pivotal moment of the novel, when Myrtle is killed by Gatsby's "rich cream color" car, but as a point of social commentary throughout the text (p. 77).

At the first of Gatsby's parties that Nick attends, there is a scene on the host's driveway as the guests are leaving, when a drunk driver runs his car off into a ditch. It is, of course, a foreshadowing of the recklessness that will cause the death of Myrtle, even up to the point of some confusion as to which drunken individual has been driving. However, as well as a structural feature of the text that echoes future events, the episode is also thematically significant as it draws attention to a growing selfishness that Fitzgerald perceives in American society. In this postwar world, there is an increasing failure on the part of the individual to recognize their responsibility toward others. Amid the drunken discussions as partygoers stand around the damaged vehicle, bystanders shout, "Well, if you are a poor driver you oughtn't to drive at night" (Fitzgerald 2019, p. 66). Why being a poor driver would make anyone a suitable daytime driver is not made clear. Owl Eyes—one of the occupants of the car—asserts the accident just "happened," implying that the behavior of actual individuals was irrelevant. This refusal to accept responsibility for one's own actions or afford responsibility to the guilty pervades the novel. As the crashed car blocks the road, other party guests remain in their cars, hooting their horns in frustration. Not much thought is given to the potential harm caused by this level of irresponsibility despite the backdrop of the carnage on American roads.

The question of dangerous drivers continues toward the end of Chapter Three when Nick has a conversation with Jordan about her poor driving. He asserts she should be more careful; however, Jordan's reply again puts the onus of responsibility not on her but on some ill-defined other, "Well other people are [careful] . . . They'll keep out of my way," she insisted. "It takes two to make an accident" (p. 71). When Nick points out that perhaps she will meet someone as careless as she, her only reflection is, "I hope I never will" (p. 72). There is no epiphany of realization that her actions could have devastating consequences for others or that she needs to moderate her behavior. Such changes it would seem should be undertaken by others, not by herself. This attitude foreshadows the response that both Tom and Daisy demonstrate in the aftermath of first Myrtle's and then Gatsby's death. They too are described by Nick as "careless." It is an interesting choice of an almost trivial word in light of the carnage they unleash on those around them. But it is also the perfect word as it suggests the sense of entitlement in—and the obliviousness of—Tom and Daisy and the extremely wealthy class they represent.

CHARACTERS

Alongside the main characters in *The Great Gatsby,* Fitzgerald created a cast of minor characters who appear in only a handful of scenes. Klipspringer, Owl Eyes, and Meyer Wolfshiem are made memorable through effective but economic description of physical appearance, action, and dialogue. The guests at Gatsby's parties, such as the movie star and her director, the gossips who speculate on their host's origins, as well as the neighbors who attend Myrtle's party at the New York apartment, all contribute to Fitzgerald's ambivalent presentation of the energy and excitement of the decade. Dr. T. J. Eckleburg is a presence that hangs over the valley of ashes without saying word—a billboard that watches over all the events and is equated with a moral force that is powerless to intervene.

The central characters who drive the plot both contrast and mirror each other. Myrtle's energy and vitality are contrasted with Daisy's languidness. Tom's self-confidence and sense of entitlement are at odds with Gatsby's insecurity and desire for approval. Myrtle's desire for a different life is mirrored in Gatsby's pursuit of Daisy. Importantly, the characters are presented to the reader through the eyes of the narrator, Nick Carraway, who is recounting events in the aftermath of the tragedy. He knows the outcome of the actions taken by them all and is—retrospectively—assigning blame.

Jay Gatsby

In a letter dated August 9, 1925, F. Scott Fitzgerald wrote to his friend John Peale Bishop about his latest novel and its eponymous hero: "You are right about Gatsby being blurred and patchy. I never at any one time saw him clear myself" (Fitzgerald 1994, p. 126). These remarks echoed the concerns raised by Fitzgerald's editor, Max Perkins, when he first read the novel before its publication: "Gatsby is somewhat vague. The reader's eyes can never quite focus upon him, his outlines are dim" (p. 87). Despite Fitzgerald's introduction of Gatsby's smile, his verbal affectation of "old sport," and his colorful shirts and suits, Gatsby remains a mysterious and blurred figure. This, of course, is the point, working as both a plot device and thematically throughout the text.

The mysterious figure of Jay Gatsby is what drives the opening section of the novel. Given the book's title, the reader is immediately aware that it is this character that is central to the story. This is reenforced by the elegiac ruminations of the narrator in the opening paragraphs of the text. We know something terrible has happened to this man but the question, "what has happened?" remains. In the opening chapter only passing references are made to Gatsby until Nick sees him in the final paragraph of the chapter stretching his arms out across the bay. Details of his life start to emerge, but they are unclear and Nick's initial impressions of him are based on rumor. First, at the party at Myrtle's apartment in Chapter Two, her sister, Catherine, claims "he's a nephew or a cousin of Kaiser Wilhelm's" and that she "is scared of him" (p. 39). This is followed by the stories circulating in Gatsby's garden during the first of his neighbor's parties that Nick attends. There is speculation among his own guests that "he killed a man" or that "he was a German spy during the war" (p. 53).

It is only in Chapter Four—approximately a third of the way through the novel—that Nick hears Gatsby's story from the man himself. However, this does not mean that what Nick is told is plausible. Gatsby tells a flamboyant tale in which he states that he was "the son of some wealthy people in the Middle West—all dead now." When Nick asked where in the Middle West, Gatsby's peculiar reply is, "San Francisco" (p. 78). He inherits considerable wealth and spends time living in the major capitals of Europe, where he was "collecting jewels, chiefly rubies, hunting big game, painting a little" (p. 79). Gatsby's "solemn" tone and the outlandishness of his story leads Nick to think that the man is teasing him before realizing that he is serious. Nick has to repress his laughter. "The very phrases were worn so threadbare that they evoked no image except that of a turbaned 'character' leaking sawdust at every pore as he pursued a tiger through the Bois de Boulogne" (p. 79).

However, Nick's belief that Gatsby is little more than an elaborate storyteller alters when he hears the stories of Gatsby's experiences during the war. His tale of battlefield bravery is given an air of authenticity when he produces a medal awarded to him by Montenegro dedicated to him and inscribed "For Valour Extraordinary" (p. 80). At the same time, he provides a photograph of himself in the quad of Trinity College, Oxford, suggesting some truth in his assertion that he had studied at the English university, an idea that both Nick and Jordan have taken to be a lie.

After the catastrophe of Myrtle's death, Nick becomes privy to the complete truth about his neighbor as "'Jay Gatsby' had broken up like glass against Tom's hard malice" (p. 177). However, structurally Fitzgerald has this information revealed at the beginning of Chapter Six providing sympathetic clarity for the reader in the midst of all those troubling and contradictory rumors. The truth of his past is more mundane than the lavish stories previously told by him and about him, but it also reveals a particularly American story.

Born James Gatz to "shiftless and unsuccessful farm people" in North Dakota he is unsatisfied with what life has bequeathed him. He leaves James Gatz behind and renames himself Jay Gatsby, the first step in his reinvention (p. 118). He headed to the south shore of Lake Superior, eking out a living as "a clam-digger and a salmon-fisher or in any other capacity that brought him food and bed" (p. 118). However, "his heart was in a constant turbulent riot" and a "universe of ineffable gaudiness spun itself out in his brain while the clock ticked on the nightstand and the moon soaked with wet light his tangled clothes upon the floor" (p. 119). He is restless, seeking opportunity, and determined to create a life worthy of his imagination. Just as that other dissatisfied farm boy, Abraham Lincoln, went from the log cabin to the White House so Jay Gatsby wants to take advantage of the American belief that an individual's destiny is a matter of self-determination. What is intriguing is that—unlike the trajectory of Abe Lincoln—Gatsby's vision of himself from this earliest of beginnings is not linked to action. It is passive. Almost as if he was waiting for something to happen. He headed to a Lutheran college but determined it was indifferent to "the drums of his destiny" and wandered back to Lake Superior, where fate throws him in the path of Dan Cody. His experience with Cody sailing the high seas, as well as being swindled out of his rightful inheritance when Cody dies, ensures that the "vague contour" of Gatsby has taken on the "substantiality of a man" (p. 121).

It is this man, penniless but conscious through his experience with Cody that anything is possible, who meets Daisy in 1917 as recounted by Jordan retrospectively. In perhaps the most extraordinary moment in the novel we see—albeit through the consciousness, indeed, the imagination of Nick Carraway—Gatsby surrender his pursuit of genuine, individualistic, perhaps even American, self-realization in order to "forever wed his unutterable visions to her perishable breath" (p. 134). The dream has transformed into one that is invested in another rather than in oneself. It is more concerned with the social recognition that comes with marrying the "golden girl" in the form of Daisy Fay, than it is about individual identity and personal achievement. In pursuit of Daisy, he returns after his wartime success with the single intention of getting money in any way possible in order to win her back. He is under the mistaken apprehension that money and its crass display is enough to make him an equivalent of the Tom Buchanans of this world. He is, of course, utterly wrong.

After Gatsby begins to realize his error in the aftermath of the party attended by Tom and Daisy, he asserts to Nick that you can "repeat the past" (p. 133). Despite Gatsby's expressed intention to wed Daisy from her family home in Louisville, literally replacing Tom Buchanan and by doing so obliterating the previous four years, Nick articulates on Gatsby's behalf a deeper, more profound desire. "He talked a lot about the past, and I gathered that he wanted to recover something, some idea of himself perhaps, that had gone into loving Daisy" (p. 133). What he has lost in his love for Daisy, is his sense of purpose that "he could climb to it . . . if he climbed alone." In a conscious moment he chooses to let his imagination "never romp again like the mind of God" and instead he kisses the girl, investing in her every hope and desire; she becomes the unworthy incarnation of his dream.

Of course, no one could be worthy because the price he has paid for her is self-betrayal. This is what he seeks to rectify when he wants to relive the past; he wants to make a different choice. From the moment he chose Daisy "[h]is life had been confused and disordered . . . but if he could once return to a certain place and go over it all slowly, he could find out what that thing was . . ." (p. 133). It is, however, too late. Toward the end of the novel, Nick envisages the possibility that Gatsby—in the moments before his death and waiting for a phone call that never came—knew it too. "[H]e must have felt that he had lost the old warm world, paid a high price for living too long with a single dream. He must have looked up at an unfamiliar sky through frightening leaves and shivered as he found what a grotesque thing a rose is and how raw the sunlight was upon the scarcely created grass" (p. 194).

In this respect Gatsby can be read as an incarnation of America itself. Striving but—at least for now—failing to live up to its promise. Seduced by the hierarchies and social conventions of Europe, identifying success with money, happiness with societal approval and celebrity, the great promise of America has been forgotten in Fitzgerald's cynical depiction of the country in the 1920s. However, the hope remained then, and it remains now, as Fitzgerald articulates in the beautiful closing sentences of his masterpiece when he merges his flawed hero with a nation. Just as Fitzgerald believed in the idea of America so "Gatsby believed in the green light, the orgastic future that year by year recedes before us. It eluded us then, but that's no matter—tomorrow we will run faster, stretch out our arms farther. . . . And one fine morning—" (p. 218).

Daisy Buchanan

On the final pages of *The Great Gatsby*, narrator Nick Carraway makes the following assertion that "[t]hey were careless people, Tom and Daisy—they smashed up things and creatures and then retreated back into their money or their vast carelessness, or whatever it was that kept them together, and let other people clean up the mess . . ." (Fitzgerald 2019, p. 216). The reader's last impression of Daisy is as one-half of a couple who have been involved with the death of both Myrtle and Gatsby and the source of Nick's need for "the world to be in uniform and at a sort of moral attention forever" (p. 2). She is presented as a beautiful, selfish destroyer of men who was too self-absorbed to send "a message or a flower" to Gatsby's funeral (p. 210). However, despite this final and lasting impression of Daisy, and the belief of some critics that she is representative of Fitzgerald's and his society's misogynistic attitude toward women, she is more complex and can be read more sympathetically than this final appearance allows.

Daisy's first appearance in the novel occurs in Chapter One when she hosts a dinner party with her husband, Tom, for Nick Carraway and Jordan Baker. She is presented in the scene as a rather childish, insincere young woman. She refers to Nick as "an absolute rose," a comparison he dismisses in his narration as "untrue. I am not faintly like a rose" (p. 18). He also refers to the quality of her voice which is "low" and "thrilling" but its hypnotic power is based on its sound rather than the words spoken. Nick initially uses a simile of music to describe it as "an arrangement of notes that will never be played again" as well as having a "singing compulsion" (p. 11). However, her hypnotic powers are destroyed "[t]he instant her voice broke off, ceasing to compel my attention, my belief, I felt the basic insincerity of what she had said" (p. 21). Her charms are spell-like, almost those of a witch who is tempter and destroyer.

However, even in this early scene we see a woman who is in a marriage that is not happy. The reader is introduced to Tom's casual carelessness and propensity for violence—unintentional or otherwise—that will be brought to bear on Myrtle when he breaks her nose in their New York love nest. Daisy points out her own "knuckle [that] was black and blue," she then states, "I know you didn't mean to, but you *did* do it" (p. 15). Tom's infidelity is also revealed in this opening chapter, and Daisy is fully aware of it. When Tom is called away to the telephone to take a call from Myrtle during dinner, she waits for a moment and then "threw her napkin on the table and excused herself and went into the house" (p. 18). When the couple return to the table after Jordan and Nick have strained to overhear her "subdued impassioned murmur," Daisy speaks with "tense gayety" (pp. 18–19).

The humiliation of this affair, still comparatively early in the marriage, is, however, not the first and—undoubtedly—will not be the last. During Jordan Baker's conversation with Nick, when she asks him to invite Daisy to tea so she can be reunited with Gatsby, she reveals that shortly after the couple's honeymoon, Tom was caught with a Santa Barbara hotel chambermaid. Further details of his betrayals are revealed when Nick's uncertainty as to why the couple had left Chicago and come East is clarified by Daisy in the confrontation scene at the Plaza Hotel. She looks at Nick and states, "[d]o you know why we left Chicago? I'm surprised that they didn't treat you to the story of that little spree" (p. 158).

Daisy is a betrayed and humiliated wife, but importantly she is also a woman with very few options that her access to money masks. She has been prepared for no other role than society debutante and society wife. Even if she decided to leave Tom, it would have real implications for her social position, which in reality is all that she has. The question she asks in her home before the fateful trip to New York could just as well apply to her entire life and not just to that hot summer day: "What'll we do with ourselves this afternoon?" cried Daisy. "And the day after that, and the next thirty years?" (p. 141). The fact that a betrayed and unhappy woman took solace in the arms of a man who adored her is, perhaps, not entirely surprising or deserving of complete condemnation.

However, as we have seen in his final reflections on Daisy and Tom, Nick does condemn her and through his immersive narration, the reader is compelled to condemn her too. We see her through his eyes as he looks retrospectively on the events of the summer. He knows, unlike the reader, what is going to happen and his knowledge colors the depiction of Daisy. By dismantling Nick's meditations on the events, it is possible to see Fitzgerald's simultaneously sympathetic and frustrated depiction of American womanhood. Perhaps the best example of this is in the Plaza Hotel when she is confronted with both her present and past as Tom and Gatsby fight for emotional and physical ownership of her. Tom's tactics are clear to see and make Daisy appear insincere and a snob. Tom reveals all the details he has discovered about Gatsby since his suspicions were first aroused. He exposes him as a "bootlegger," a fact Gatsby does not deny. He reveals that Gatsby had left Walter Chase "in the lurch" and "let him go to jail for a month," he has broken "the betting laws" and is now involved in something that "Walter's afraid" to tell Tom about and all the while Daisy "was staring terrified between Gatsby and her husband" (p. 161).

Terrified of what exactly? Undoubtedly, the growing threat of potential physical violence between the pair. Terrified of the emotional outpourings that will have undetermined ramifications going forward. But also, possibly, terrified of Gatsby who has been revealed as very different from the man she had once known. Unaware of where her lover has earned his money, and used to people inheriting theirs, she is confronted for the first time with his criminality. The horror of this realization is not simultaneously experienced by the reader who has been told by Nick at the outset that "Gatsby turned out all right in the end; it is what preyed on Gatsby, what foul dust floated in the wake of his dreams that temporarily closed out my interest in the abortive sorrows and short-winded elations of men" (p. 3). Therefore, in Nick's subjective telling, Gatsby is a victim and Daisy rejects him not because of his criminality but because of her snobbery.

However, Daisy is not only browbeaten by Tom, she does not fare much better at the hands of Gatsby. Not satisfied that Daisy loves him now, he insists that she wipe out her relationship with Tom and deny that she ever loved him at all. Reminded of happier times by her husband, she refuses to lie to her-self, Gatsby, or Tom about her past and her relationships with both men. This is not enough for Gatsby who responds to her assertion that she had loved him as well as Tom with a disbelieving, "[y]ou loved me *too*?" Tom takes the opportunity to add more misery to the situation by declaring, "[e]ven that's a lie" (p. 159). Significantly neither man respects nor even sees that she has had experiences—as well as an internal life—that is separate from them. They cannot see her as anything other than an extension of themselves.

Daisy's lack of agency, her inability to make a decision in the confrontation between Tom and Gatsby, and her desire to escape the situation she has triggered result in her appeal to her husband: "*Please* Tom! I can't stand this any-more!" (p. 162). With this direct appeal, Tom takes control and Gatsby is all but defeated. This is mirrored by her behavior after the death of Myrtle where she again defers to her husband's plan at their kitchen table as seen by Nick and presented by him as weakness and carelessness. However, it can also be seen as the by-product of a society that infantilizes women but simultaneously blames them when they are unable to take moral responsibility for their actions. In Fitzgerald's construction of Daisy, filtered through the eyes of Nick, it is pos-sible to see his own ambivalence to modern womanhood—simultaneously enthralled and terrified by it.

Tom Buchanan

In a letter dated November 20, 1924, Max Perkins wrote to Fitzgerald, "I would know Tom Buchanan if I met him on the street and I would avoid him" (Fitz-gerald 1994, p. 87). This attests to the vividness with which Tom is drawn in comparison to the more elusive Gatsby or ghostly George Wilson. Along with

Meyer Wolfshiem, he is given the most detailed physical description of any of the characters in the book. The reader's introduction to Tom in Chapter One is focused on his "cruel body" and its power, reflecting both his physical and social dominance (Fitzgerald 2019, p. 8). However, this is undercut by reference to "the effeminate swank of his riding clothes," his "acute limited excellence at twenty-one," and his wistful pursuit of "the dramatic turbulence of some irrecoverable football game" (p. 7). For all his physical prowess, throughout the course of the novel he is portrayed as a man who does not do anything, a man whose best days are well and truly behind him. When Gatsby introduces him to other guests at one of his parties, the only means of identifying what he does is to refer to him as "the polo player," much to Tom's chagrin. Fitzgerald further emphasizes his wealth but lack of meaningful action in the absence of any reference to his war record; the tacit implication is that Tom did not serve, in contrast to Gatsby and Nick whose first conversation identified their shared military service.

Tom's social authority, rooted in his wealth and family name, is revealed as absurd when his intellectual, psychological, and emotional shortcomings are unveiled. At the dinner held at the Buchanan residence in the opening chapter, Tom's rant about race and civilization prompted by his reading of Goddard's *The Rise of the Colored Empires* exposes his inability to express the ideas of somebody else let alone articulate, or even form, his own. His irrational assertions also demonstrate his fear that his position as a wealthy white man is in some way under threat in a world that is rapidly changing.

Similarly, his shock and confusion when he is "astounded" to realize the nature of the relationship between his wife and Gatsby shows emotional and psychological limitations (p. 142). He was unable to foresee the possibility that Daisy, humiliated by his numerous affairs, should seek "to have something in her life" as Jordan suggests (p. 96). His response to the affair is that of a petulant child. There is a confrontation with the man whom he sees has taken something that belongs to him followed by an assertion of ownership. He seems less concerned with Daisy's affair per se than with the fact that it was conducted with "Mr. Nobody from Nowhere." Indeed, he ties such relationships with the collapse of civilization and associates it with the—albeit slow—changing attitudes toward race: "Nowadays people begin by sneering at family life and family institutions, and next they'll throw everything overboard and have intermarriage between black and white" (p.156). No consideration is given on a personal level to the implications of the emotional and physical betrayals that have entered the Buchanan marriage. Tom dismisses his own affairs as "a spree" during which he loves his wife "all the time," to which Daisy responds, "[y]ou're revolting" (p. 158).

Tom's emotional immaturity is on display again in the aftermath of Myrtle's death. Although he responds to her demise with grief, his means of expression are again the responses of an angry child or hurt animal. After leaving the garage where Tom has seen his mistress's corpse and returning to his car, Nick hears "a low husky sob, and saw that the tears were overflowing down his face." His response then quickly turns to rage, and his focus to the man he believes has attempted—and this time succeeded—in taking something else from him, "The God Damn coward!" he whimpered. "He didn't even stop his car" (p. 170). When, some weeks later, Nick sees Tom for the last time on Fifth Avenue as he attempts to justify his role in the deaths of Gatsby and George the same lack of emotional depth is on display. "And if you think I didn't have my share of suffering—look here, when I went to give up that flat and saw that damn box of dog biscuits sitting there on the sideboard, I sat down and cried like a baby. By God it was awful——" (p. 216). At this point, Nick's attitude to Tom changes. He says that he can neither like nor forgive him, but he recognizes that in Tom's mind all his actions were justified. "I shook hands with him; it seemed silly not to, for I felt suddenly as though I were talking to a child" (p. 216).

Equating Tom with a child is significant. This man-child not only does not—and cannot—accept responsibility for his actions, he is not even asked to do so as demonstrated by Nick shaking his hand in their final meeting. To this extent, Nick too becomes culpable in the carnage representing the culpability of all American society. Nick reflects that "[t]hey were careless people, Tom and Daisy—they smashed up things and creatures and then retreated back into their money or their vast carelessness or whatever it was that kept them together, and let other people clean up the mess they had made . . ." (p. 216). In some respects, the damning indictment is as much on those that clean up after them as it is on Tom and Daisy.

Myrtle Wilson

In many respects, Myrtle Wilson represents the same ambitions and dreams as Jay Gatsby. She, like the novel's hero, strives to reinvent herself but—again like Gatsby—she is unable to fully articulate what that reinvention should be. In this void of purpose, she attaches her dreams to money, popular culture, and her adulterous relationship with Tom.

Myrtle is introduced to the reader in the garage run by her husband, George, in the bleak valley of ashes. The lifelessness exhibited by George is contrasted with Myrtle's "perceptible vitality." Fitzgerald subtly aligns her with Gatsby when Nick observes that this vitality was "as if the nerves of her body were continually smouldering" (Fitzgerald 2019, p. 30). A similar sensitivity is present in the description of Gatsby at the opening of the novel where Nick describes him as having "some heightened sensitivity to the promises of life, as if he were related to one of those intricate machines that register earthquakes ten thousand miles away" (p. 2).

However, the vapidness of Myrtle's attempts at social climbing are evident throughout the apartment that Tom keeps for her in New York in order for the pair to conduct their affair. The apartment is small, but the furniture is too large for it. Myrtle herself is presented as being too full of life and energy for the confines of the space, perhaps suggesting the emotional and social limitations that remain in place despite her involvement with Tom. The restrictions that make genuine change impossible—in part because of the short-sighted inability of Myrtle to see the supposed possibility of America and, oxymoronically, because such possibilities are not really open to her—are clear when Nick identifies the difference between her persona in the apartment and how she appeared in the Wilsons' garage. The vitality that was rooted in her physicality and movement—so at odds with the languid Daisy—is transmuted in this small apartment into "impressive hauteur" as "[h]er laughter, her gestures, her assertions became more violently affected moment by moment" (Fitzgerald 2019, p. 36). She performs in a manner she believes to be suitable for the setting she misperceives as sophisticated. There are regular costume changes, dismissals of compliments about her clothes, and disdain for "the lower orders" (p. 38). There are copies of celebrity scandal magazines, and a best-selling but controversial novel, *Simon Called Peter* (1921), littering the apartment. In some respects, this space has become a microcosm for all that modern America has to offer; celebrity instead of art; controversy instead of insight; and performance rather than substance. Myrtle has embraced it all.

Of course, she will be destroyed by the modern world that she has misunderstood just as Gatsby is sacrificed on its altar. Both are victims of their belief that external trappings and social relationships can construct new identities that are worthy of their great hopes and aspirations to be other than they are. Trapped in the valley of ashes, as her husband's suspicions mount, Myrtle—believing that Tom is driving Gatsby's car—runs out into the road and is killed by that symbol of the modern world—the automobile. Her death, if depicted in the nineteenth century, would have been punishment for her adultery. However, Fitzgerald suggests her death is the result of the shortcomings of an industrialized modern America that is perhaps not so very different from the aristocratic European world that it was supposed to exceed. The description of her death emphasizes her lost—indeed her wasted—energy. "The mouth was wide open and ripped at the corners, as though she had choked a little in giving up the tremendous vitality she had stored so long". The description of "her left breast swinging loose like a flap" will be echoed at the end of the novel and in many respects undermines Nick's reveries about the dream that inspired American beginnings (p. 165). He reflects on "a fresh, green breast of the new world" that was the last time man came "face to face for the last time in history with something commensurate to his capacity for wonder" (pp. 217–218). The images alongside one another demonstrate that this new world is not so very different from the old.

George Wilson

The contrast between Myrtle Wilson and her husband George is startling. Myrtle's vitality and color are emphasized by her husband's ghostlike grayness; he is presented as almost part of the valley of ashes as opposed to being one of its residents. He is described as "mingling immediately with the cement color of the walls. A white ashen dust veiled his dark suit and his pale hair as it veiled everything in the vicinity" (p. 30). The garage itself is described as "a shadow" (p. 29) and his wife, who is the only thing not veiled in dust, walks "through her husband as if he were a ghost" (p. 30).

However, just as Myrtle sees Tom as a way out of the frustrations of her life, so, in fact, does George. Nick recounts that "[w]hen he saw us a damp gleam of hope sprang into his light blue eyes" (p. 29). George wants to buy a car from Tom in order to sell it. The interaction between the two shows the power Tom has over—not only George—but most, in fact all, men. The desire for the car will reemerge toward the end of the novel, when Tom momentarily seems to lose control over events as—immediately after realizing the nature of the relationship between Daisy and Gatsby—he encounters a more assertive George as the party leaves Long Island and heads to the full-blown confrontation at the Plaza Hotel. George again asks for the car so he can "go West," the symbol in the American psyche of new frontiers and opportunities, freedom and new beginnings, the possibility of reinvention. Of course, George doesn't realize he is too late. The Old West is dead as the New America has consumed everything in its wake. He will not go west; there will be no new beginning. He will be a pawn in Tom's game of asserting dominance over his wife, Gatsby, and the publicized narrative of events. Lied to by Tom, George seeks out Gatsby and emerges "an ashen fantastic figure gliding toward him through the amorphous trees," killing him before killing himself (p. 194).

Jordan Baker

Fitzgerald takes another opportunity to explore modern womanhood through Jordan Baker. Although young and beautiful, she is different from her friend Daisy Buchanan in significant ways. First, she is unmarried, allowing her to enjoy the increased freedoms offered to women after the First World War far more than Daisy. She attends a number of Gatsby's parties and she has the freedom to spend time with Nick, among other men including the "persistent undergraduate given to violent innuendo" who accompanies her to the first of Gatsby's parties that Nick attends (p. 54). Jordan also has an occupation—something clearly lacking in Daisy's life—as a professional golfer. This makes her both financially independent and free to travel around the country. Her status as an unmarried and fatherless woman also means that she can operate beyond the reaches of familial patriarchal structures that could curtail her. When Tom asserts that her family "oughtn't to let her run around the country this way," Daisy points out that her family consists of "one aunt about a thousand years old" (p. 23). This lack of male control over Jordan terrifies Tom and his anxiety about female independence reappears when he queries how Gatsby knew his wife. "I wonder where in the devil he met Daisy. By God, I may be old-fashioned in my ideas, but women run around too much these days to suit me. They meet all kinds of crazy fish" (p. 125).

However, despite the presentation of Jordan as an independent, modern woman it is riddled with ambivalence. In this depiction of postwar female emancipation, Fitzgerald introduces doubt about the integrity of her character almost immediately. At the dinner party in Chapter One, when Nick realizes who Jordan is, he remembers that he "had heard some story of her too, a critical, unpleasant story, but what it was I had forgotten long ago" (p. 23). However, he remembers during the course of the summer when he is conscious of a lie she told about leaving "a car out in the rain with the top down." He recalls that she was at the center of an episode "that approached the proportions of a scandal" and almost "reached the newspapers" in which during her first major tournament there was a suggestion "that she had moved her ball from a bad lie in the semi-final round" (p. 70). Nick seems more troubled by Jordan's small-scale cheating than by Meyer Wolfshiem's fixing of the 1919 World Series, which only results in Nick being "staggered" (p. 88). However, Jordan's dishonesty is not a particular concern for Nick. According to him "[d]ishonesty in a woman is a thing you never blame deeply" (p. 71).

Jordan's independence is undercut throughout the novel by her infantilization by Nick and by implication by Fitzgerald. She cheats to win a game and she lies to avoid responsibility in the manner of a child. Nick, in paternalistic fashion, forgives her these shortcomings but at the end of the novel she is condemned in the same way as Daisy. It would seem whether a woman is independent like Jordan or trapped in traditional family roles like Daisy she is the source of male unease and, in some cases, destruction. At the end of the novel, Nick forgives Gatsby his storytelling and fabrications as part of his "conception of himself" (p.118) and even shakes hands with Tom but Jordan leaves Nick "angry" and "tremendously sorry" (p. 214).

Nick Carraway

It is through the narrator, Nick Carraway, that the story of Jay Gatsby—his creation and destruction—is told. However, it is worth remembering that this narrator does more than tell the story, he also mediates and imagines it. This is indicated in the opening paragraphs when the reader is introduced to the idea that Nick is doing far more than documenting the summer of 1922; he is telling his story for a reason. This compulsion is, perhaps, reminiscent of the motivations of the narrator in Samuel Taylor Coleridge's "The Rime of the Ancient Mariner" (1798), who is also compelled to tell a story of wrongdoing in an attempt to absolve himself from his own involvement in it.

Nick states that, "[w]hen I came back from the East last autumn I felt that I wanted the world to be in uniform and at a sort of moral attention forever" (Fitzgerald 2019, p. 2). However, his craving for old certainties is not only the result of what he witnessed (and was involved in) through the summer of 1922, it also lies in what motivated Nick to go East that year in the first place. "I participated in that delayed Teutonic migration known as the Great War. I enjoyed the counter-raid so thoroughly that I came back restless" (p. 3). The chaos and meaningless of the war led to his questioning of the world to which he returned. He asserts that, "instead of being the warm center of the world, the Middle West now seemed like the ragged edge of the universe" (p. 3). Of course, it is not his home that has changed, it is he. This backdrop of the war is significant. The America that Fitzgerald presents in the novel—its recklessness, its chaotic fun, its changing gender and race relations, is, to a large extent, the product of the war.

The opening paragraphs also reveal Nick in all his complexity and—at times—reveals his lack of self-awareness, factors that will deeply affect and complicate the manner of his narration. The novel opens with Nick reflecting on advice given to him by his father. "'Whenever you feel like criticizing anyone,' he told me, 'just remember that all the people in this world haven't had the advantages that you've had'" (p. 1). Nick then claims that he has always reserved judgment, which is a suggestion that is undermined through the course of the novel and even on the same page as his assertion. However, he also shows himself as having misunderstood his father's meaning when at the end of these early reflections he says, "I am still a little afraid of missing something if I forget that, as my father snobbishly suggested, and I snobbishly repeat, a sense of the fundamental decencies is parceled out unequally at birth" (p. 2). His father's meaning is misinterpreted; Carraway Senior is concerned with the advantages afforded to some in terms of money, education, and security in comparison to those who have not been born into such situations. Nick's interpretation is that people like him are born with a greater sense of morality and decency than those who are not like him. In some respects, Nick's remarks can be seen as endorsing the status quo that privileges some at the expense of others, simply by accident of birth.

A significant factor in the construction of Nick Carraway is his double role as both observer of events and participant. In many respects, the retrospective nature as well as the tone of Nick's narration, encourages the reader to perceive Nick as a bystander to the events that unfold rather than actively engaged in them. However, on closer examination it becomes clear that this is categorically not the case. Nick is involved whether he chooses to admit it or not. Alongside Nick the narrator is Nick the participant. He is crucial in the reunification of Gatsby and Daisy; he is privy to the details of the affairs of both Gatsby and Daisy and Tom and Myrtle; and most important—despite his moral outrage that casts a shadow over the opening paragraphs of the novel—he is pivotal in ensuring that the truth about Gatsby and his death is not revealed at the time of Myrtle's inquest. He clears up, or rather covers up, the mess made by the Buchanans while condemning them. Just as his misinterpretation of his father's advice reveals a desire to maintain the status quo, so does his failure to clear Gatsby's name in the aftermath of his death.

One possible reading—among many—of Nick's narration is that it is driven by a desire to create meaning out of a series of events that are fundamentally meaningless. It is a search for a coherent narrative out of the chaos, as well as a plea for absolution for his own involvement in the tragedy. When Nick's elegiac narration is taken away, the events of that summer are a string of sordid affairs, violent deaths, bootlegging, criminality, and amorality. Fundamentally, there is little decency in any of these characters, and even if Nick excludes Gatsby from his condemnation, it does not automatically follow that he should. It could be argued that Gatsby is as culpable as any of the others. He is a man who involved himself with crime in order to get what he wanted, and his involvement with bootlegging is by definition involvement with violence. He obsessed over a married woman in a manner that we would now call stalking. He kept newspaper clippings of society pages in which she was featured and obtained a house opposite hers in order to be close to her. He fabricated his life story, had an affair with a married woman, and tried to cover up the details of Myrtle's death. However, the only way that the story can make sense for Nick is to make Gatsby the hero of it. He is the innocent destroyed by the narcissism of the Buchanans and the corruption of America in the 1920s. After the meaningless destruction of World War One, Nick Carraway needs this mess to make sense.

Many of the emotions and reflections attributed to Gatsby are actually conjured up by Nick. For example, in the aftermath of the party attended by both of the Buchanans, Gatsby tells Nick about his love for Daisy, his previous relationship with her, and his anxieties. Gatsby worries that Daisy was unimpressed with the party, "[s]he didn't like it." He also asserts that, "[s]he didn't have a good time" and "I feel far away from her . . . [i]t's hard to make her understand" (p. 133). His speech, in this scene and throughout the novel as a whole, is straightforward and matter of fact. After this conversation Nick summarizes what Gatsby has told him about the early days of his relationship with Daisy. It is hard to believe that this man with his "old sport" affectation, who had provoked barely suppressed "incredulous laughter" (p. 79) on the part of Nick when recounting his fictitious past, would be the same man who would desire to "suck on the pap of life, gulp down the incomparable milk of wonder" or speak of "the tuning-fork that had been struck upon a star" (p. 134). It also seems unlikely that anything that Gatsby would have said would inspire Nick's reflections that "I was reminded of something—an elusive rhythm, a fragment of lost words, that I had heard somewhere a long time ago [but] . . . what I had almost remembered was uncommunicable forever" (p. 134). It would appear that as Gatsby has projected his dream of self-invention on to Daisy, so Nick has projected his search for a coherent narrative on to Gatsby.

FURTHER READING

Berman, R. 1994. The Great Gatsby *and Modern Times*. Urbana: University of Illinois Press.

Churchwell, S. 2014. *Careless People: Murder, Mayhem and the Invention of* The Great Gatsby. London: Virago.

Long, R. 1979. *The Achieving of* The Great Gatsby*: F. Scott Fitzgerald, 1920–1925*. Lewisburg, Pa.: Bucknell University Press.

FURTHER VIEWING

Fitzgerald's 1995 handwritten manuscript held at Princeton University can be viewed at https://findingaids.princeton.edu/collections/C0187/c00019.

Hazard, B., M. Corrigan, M. Cotey, D. Ault, and R. S. Williams. "Gatsby in Connecticut: Reimagining Gatsby." Webinar from ATG Communications, May 15, 2020. https://vimeo.com/419374182.

Luhrmann, B., dir. *The Great Gatsby*. 2013. Los Angeles, CA: Warner Bros.

Williams, R. S., dir. *Gatsby in Connecticut*. 2020. Dallas, TX: Against the Grain Productions.

FURTHER LISTENING

Bragg, M. "The Great Gatsby." *In Our Time*. Podcast audio. January 14, 2021. Accessed February 1, 2021. https://www.bbc.co.uk/programmes/m000r4tq.

Chapter 5

Later Novels: *Tender Is the Night* (1934) and *The Last Tycoon* (1941)

Fitzgerald's later novels are often looked at through the prism of the personal difficulties that the author was experiencing during their composition. It is tempting as a reader to get absorbed in the biography of the Fitzgeralds, which reads almost as a novel in itself. However, *Tender Is the Night* should be viewed as an artistic achievement that—although different from *The Great Gatsby*—is its equal. Thematically, it is complex in its exploration of madness, sexual abuse, coercion, addiction, identity, and trauma. It is a fascinating novel to explore in the present moment when many of these issues are being discussed and confronted openly for the first time.

The Last Tycoon, although unfinished, can be viewed as an early example of a work in a new American genre: the Hollywood novel. Alongside Nathanael West's *The Day of the Locust* (1939), Budd Schulberg's *What Makes Sammy Run?* (1941), and Evelyn Waugh's *The Loved One* (1948), Fitzgerald, in this novel, decided to write about Hollywood instead of for it.

TENDER IS THE NIGHT: COMPOSITION

The composition of *Tender Is the Night* is probably the most complex of any of Fitzgerald's novels. This is largely because of the lengthy period of composition as well as the number of plots and drafts, starts and abandonments, that the author made. Such is the complexity, Fitzgerald scholar Matthew J. Bruccoli wrote in a 250-page book on the subject. *The Composition of* Tender Is the Night (1963) charts the various versions and redrafts undertaken by Fitzgerald in the nine years that he took to bring the novel to completion. However, despite the repeated assertion that the book was nine years in the making, a closer look makes it clear that this is not strictly accurate. It certainly did take Fitzgerald nine years to publish another book after *The Great Gatsby*, but to suggest that *Tender Is the Night* is the same book that Fitzgerald began in 1925 is misleading.

Fitzgerald's initial plans for a new novel in 1925 are detailed in letters to both Max Perkins and his literary agent Harold Ober. Writing to Perkins only weeks after the publication of *Gatsby* he expressed his excitement about his new project. "The happiest thought I have is of my new novel—it is something really NEW in form, idea, structure—the model for the age that Joyce and Stien [sic] are searching for, that Conrad didn't find" (Fitzgerald 1994, p. 108). An enthusiastic and confident assertion, perhaps he was riding on the wave of his artistic success with *Gatsby* in the weeks before he realized that it had not been as commercially successful as he had hoped. His subject matter would be something of a departure from his previous work as it would be focused on a son's killing of his mother. The real-life source of his proposed plot was sixteen-year-old Dorothy Ellingson's murder of her mother in January 1925 in San Francisco after she was refused permission to attend a dance. It was covered in a sensational and salacious manner by the press who saw it as the final destination of jazzmania. On the face of it, who better to write the cautionary tale of the 1920s than the man who—if not invented—named the Jazz Age?

Despite Fitzgerald's initial excitement, as well as the subject matter that could produce an interesting angle on America in the 1920s, progress was spluttering. Over the next seven years the book would go through a series of titles: "Our Type," "The Boy Who Killed His Mother," "The Melarkey Case," and "The World's Fair." The central character of these early versions was Francis Melarkey, a film technician, who falls under the spell of a married couple in Europe and murders his domineering mother. Some of this material did remain in the final published novel but the focus of the project radically shifted after Zelda Fitzgerald's first mental collapse in 1930. Her ill health and subsequent treatment would be a source of material for Fitzgerald, as would the increasing pressures on and the fissures in their marriage.

In 1932, the book went under a process of radical replanning, salvaging some material from previous drafts, but to a large extent Fitzgerald was beginning again. Potential titles for the novel were "The Drunkard's Holiday" and "Doctor Diver's Holiday" before Fitzgerald settled on the evocative quotation from Keats's "Ode to a Nightingale," *Tender Is the Night*. The central characters were now Dick Diver, a psychiatrist, and his wife and former patient, Nicole. The pair are initially seen through the naïve eyes of Rosemary Hoyt, a movie starlet who arrives in Europe with her forceful mother. The murder plot was dropped but the book remains full of sexual and physical violence, mental turmoil, and trauma.

TENDER IS THE NIGHT: SYNOPSIS

Book One of the novel opens with the arrival on the French Riviera of a movie starlet, eighteen-year-old Rosemary Hoyt, and her widowed mother Elsie Speers. During her first day on the beach, she meets a group of people consisting of Albert McKisco, his wife Violet, Luis Campion, and Royal Dumphry. She is, however, less interested in them than in a second, more glamorous group also frequenting the beach. A few days later she is invited to join them by Dick Diver and she is introduced to his wife, Nicole, and their friends Abe and Mary North, and Tommy Barban. Rosemary starts to fall in love with Dick.

The Divers host a party at their Villa Diana home and both of the groups are present. Rosemary tells Dick that she has fallen in love with him. Mrs. McKisco reveals that she has seen a strange event in the bathroom involving Nicole Diver during the course of the party. Before the breakup of the party, Dick asks Rosemary to go to Paris with the group to bid farewell to Abe North who is returning to America. Rosemary's mother encourages her to pursue a relationship with Dick. Luis Campion tells Rosemary that there is to be a duel between Tommy Barban and Albert McKisco. Abe North reveals that the cause of the duel is Tommy wanting Violet McKisco to stop talking about what she had witnessed at the Divers' home. The demand led to a confrontation between her husband and Barban. Rosemary goes to the duel; both men fire and both men miss.

The action then shifts to Paris where they socialize and Nicole and Rosemary shop. They also take a trip to the battlefields of Northern France where Dick reflects on the nature and the outcome of the First World War despite not having served on the frontline. Back in Paris, Rosemary begins to realize that Abe is constantly drinking. Rosemary and Dick kiss in a taxi and she invites him back to her hotel room, but he refuses. By the next day, however, Rosemary senses that Dick is developing feelings for her. The group attends a viewing of Rosemary's new film *Daddy's Girl*. She announces that she has arranged a screen test for Dick, to the amusement of the others, but he refuses. Later, he admits to Rosemary that he is falling in love with her but reveals that his relationship with Nicole is complicated and must continue.

At the Gare Saint-Lazare, Nicole meets Abe where they have a painful conversation about Abe's psychological collapse. It is also revealed to the reader that Abe has been in love with Nicole for some time. Dick, Mary North, and

Rosemary Hoyt arrive to say farewell to Abe. As his train is about to depart an acquaintance of the Divers, Maria Wallis, shoots her lover.

In the following days, Diver's jealousy is aroused by an old acquaintance of Rosemary's suggesting that she is possibly not as naïve and innocent as he may have thought. As a result, he pursues her more aggressively. The group also discovers that Abe North is still in Paris. Shortly afterward, Dick kisses Rosemary in his hotel room when Abe appears at the door with a black man, Jules Peterson, who has identified a man that he believes has robbed Abe. The wrong man has been arrested and now a number of men are after Peterson for his treachery. While Abe, Dick, and Rosemary discuss what to do, Peterson waits in the corridor. After Abe has left, Rosemary goes back to her room where she finds Peterson, murdered on her bed. Concerned about the potential damage to Rosemary's reputation, Dick moves the body into the hallway and tells the hotel manager that this is where the body was found. He takes the bloody bedsheets from Rosemary's room to his own for Nicole to clean. Rosemary sees Nicole in the midst of hysteria in the bathroom realizing what Mrs. McKisco may have seen at the party at Villa Diana.

Book Two opens with a flashback to 1917 charting the early career of Dick, now referred to as Dr. Richard Diver. After an illustrious academic career that involved study at Yale, a Rhodes scholarship, attendance at Johns Hopkins medical school, and study in Vienna, he arrives in Zurich to continue his research. His field of specialization is psychiatry. After completion he is drafted into the army, not on the frontline but in a medical capacity. After the war he returns to Zurich.

Dick visits the Dohmler clinic and tells Dr. Gregorovius about letters that he received from a wealthy patient, Nicole Warren, whom he met just before entering the military. Gregorovius relates her psychological history that reveals an incestuous relationship with her father after the death of her mother. Dick is supposedly still focused on becoming the best doctor he can be. However, his feelings for Nicole start to deepen. There are a number of attempts to end the growing relationship but to no avail. Nicole's sister, Beth (nicknamed Baby), is unhappy at the prospect of the two marrying but also seems eager to have a doctor to care for her damaged sibling.

Perspective then shifts to Nicole who through an impressionistic stream of consciousness recounts details of the Diver marriage and children, her relapses into mental ill health as well as Diver's increasing reliance on Warren money and reduced focus on his work. This passage ends at the point that the novel begins, with Nicole looking at Rosemary on the beach.

Action shifts to the aftermath of Peterson's murder. Rosemary moves to another hotel and the Divers return to the Villa Diana. On a ski trip to Gstaad, Dr. Gregorovius suggests that he and Dick set up a new clinic. The move is encouraged by Baby Warren and backed by Warren money. Some of Dick's patients are detailed as are a number of Nicole's breakdowns, one of which resulted in her grabbing the steering wheel of the car that Dick was driving and running it off the road. After her recovery, Dick heads to Munich to get away. Here he meets Tommy Barban who tells him that Abe North has been beaten to death in a New York speakeasy.

In Innsbruck, Dick reflects that he has lost himself in the time between meeting Nicole and then Rosemary. He is informed of his father's death and sails to America for the funeral. He becomes increasingly aware of his failure to fully commit to his vocation and to his responsibilities. On the return voyage he encounters Albert McKisco, now a successful novelist. Back in Europe, he heads to see Rosemary in Rome where they consummate their relationship. After a drinking spree he gets into a row with a taxi driver and is subsequently beaten by the police and arrested. He calls on Baby Warren to help him and she organizes his release.

Book Three opens with the wife of Dr. Gregorovius suggesting to her husband that Dick is no longer serious about his work. On his return to the clinic, Gregorovius sends him to Lausanne to see a potential patient. While there, he discovers Nicole's father is being treated for alcoholism and is dying. Dick summons Nicole but by the time she arrives her father has left the place. Back at the clinic, a patient is removed because his parents could smell alcohol on Dick's breath. The partnership between himself and Gregorovius is dissolved and the Divers head back to the Riviera.

At the Villa Diana, the relationship between the couple becomes increasingly fraught. Dick tries to work but with little success, and his drinking increases. Rosemary appears on the Riviera and Nicole is embarrassed by Dick's attempts to impress her on an aquaplane. She writes a seductive letter to Tommy Barban who has also been spending time with the couple. When Dick is out of town Nicole meets up with Tommy and has sex with him. Tommy demands that Dick grant Nicole a divorce, and he does.

The closing of the novel finds Nicole and Tommy married and Dick back in America where he returns to medical practice. He writes to Nicole from increasingly small towns and the final line of the novel is written from her perspective:

"Perhaps, so she liked to think, his career was biding its time, again like Grant's in Galena; his latest note was postmarked from Hornell, New York, which is some distance from Geneva and a very small town; in any case he is almost certainly in that section of the country, in one town or another" (Fitzgerald 2012a, p. 352).

TENDER IS THE NIGHT: INTERPRETATIONS

Tender Is the Night is open to multifaceted and complex readings. It is an exploration of a troubled marriage that draws upon the problems experienced between the author and his wife. It is an analysis of mental collapse in both men and women. It is a study of alcoholism, trauma, and the aftermath of war. It explores the importance of vocation and the destructive power of money when not marshaled by moral and personal responsibility.

Critics have tended to read the novel sympathetically toward either Dick Diver or Nicole Diver rather than recognizing it as a depiction of a marriage between two flawed and complex characters. One argument is that Dick Diver is destroyed by Nicole and the Warren family. The price of Nicole's return to health is not only the destruction of Diver's physical and emotional health but also the sacrifice of his vocation. The Warrens, and the exceptionally wealthy class that they represent, are vampires feeding off the decency of men like Diver who represent the very best of America. Diver is corrupted by money and love and in the process loses sight of his vocation and individual destiny.

Alternate readings focus on the autobiographical subject matter of the novel and explore how it reflects Fitzgerald's attempts to suppress Zelda's artistic endeavors and simultaneously blame her for his own shortcomings; in the portrayal of the couple, Fitzgerald's hostility toward women in general and Zelda in particular is evident. It has been read as an unconscious depiction of male anxiety around the increasing independence of women. Nicole's sister Baby Warren is held up as a figure of fear for Fitzgerald. Other readings have considered Nicole's desire to tell and control her own narrative as an exploration of women encroaching on previous male preserves of artistic expression and the fear that this generates in the male artist. This interpretation often explores Fitzgerald's anxiety at the time that Zelda published her novel, *Save Me the Waltz* (1932) and the two novels have been read in conjunction with one another.

However, this either/or approach to the central relationship depicted in the novel unjustly simplifies it. In *Tender Is the Night* Fitzgerald depicts multiple perspectives on the same events with some scenes being depicted more than once from a variety of viewpoints. The multiple perspectives are a recognition that individuals do not experience the same event—or the same relationship—in the same way. Through the course of the novel, Fitzgerald explores the fictional world from the perspective of Dick, Nicole, Rosemary, and Abe North among others. It is a novel that has a cacophony of voices representing the complexity and multiplicity of the modern world.

THE LAST TYCOON: SYNOPSIS

The novel opens with college student Cecelia Brady returning home to Hollywood for the summer vacation. On the plane she chats to screenwriter Wylie White and film executive Mannie Schwartz. They stop at Nashville but Schwartz does not get back on the flight and Cecelia finds out later that he has committed suicide. Cecelia also talks to her father's film studio business partner, Monroe Stahr, who is traveling as Mr. Smith. Cecelia is secretly in love with him and has been for many years. Schwartz has sent a note to Stahr warning him about his enemies.

A month later Cecelia is in her father's office when an earthquake occurs causing flooding on the lot. Stahr enlists the help of his troubleshooter "Robby" Robinson. While on the lot Stahr sees a woman who is the image of his dead wife and he makes plans to find out who she is.

Stahr is seen at work where he meets with screenwriters and directors. He explains his dissatisfaction with a script due to be filmed in the following weeks and advises how he thinks it could be improved. He also reveals plans to make a high-quality picture even if it involves losing money. Robinson leaves a message saying he has information about the woman from the flooded lot; her surname is Smith. Stahr has his secretary phone all Smiths newly arrived in Los Angeles. Edna Smith contacts Stahr revealing herself to be the woman from the lot. They meet and Stahr sees no resemblance to his dead wife. However, when he sees her housemate, Kathleen Moore, he realizes that she is the woman and he invites her to visit the studio. The two begin seeing each other and consummate their relationship despite Kathleen being engaged to another man, which she reveals in a letter to Stahr.

It is revealed that Stahr has heart trouble at a weekly medical examination and his doctor reflects that he will die soon. Kathleen contacts Stahr, who—still distraught by the content of the letter—agrees to meet her. They drive around in his limousine and he urges her to go away for the weekend with him, but she resists. Stahr decides to wait until the next day to persuade her that her future lies with him, but the following afternoon he receives a telegram from her telling him she had married the man at noon.

Stahr and Cecelia have dinner with Brimmer, a member of the Communist Party and he complains about interference with his scriptwriters. Distraught about the loss of Kathleen, Stahr gets uncharacteristically drunk and threatens to beat up Brimmer, but Brimmer hits him instead and knocks him to the floor. After he leaves, Stahr invites Kathleen to the ranch of Douglas Fairbanks.

This is as far as Fitzgerald got before his death on December 21, 1940. However, notes do indicate Fitzgerald's plans for the rest of the novel: Stahr would resume his affair with Kathleen after her marriage. Brady would attempt to blackmail Stahr to get him to leave the studio. In retaliation Stahr would gather incriminating information on Brady. Brady would plan to have Stahr killed, and on discovering this Stahr would arrange the murder of Brady while he was out of Hollywood. However, Stahr has a change of heart, but before he can call off the hit man, he is killed in a plane crash. Cecelia is left without her father and the man she loves.

THE LAST TYCOON: REFLECTIONS ON AN UNFINISHED NOVEL

The Last Tycoon, despite being posthumously published in 1941, was far from completion at the time of Fitzgerald's premature death. As a result, it is difficult to determine if the novel would have been a return to form for the novelist. What can be said is that what Fitzgerald did leave behind shows signs of his brilliance and flair. The opening two sentences beautifully situate the reader in the world of the novel and the perspective of Fitzgerald's young female narrator, Cecelia Brady. "Though I haven't ever been on the screen I was brought up in pictures. Rudolph Valentino came to my fifth birthday party—or so I was told. I put this down only to indicate that even before the age of reason I was in a position to watch the wheels go round" (Fitzgerald 1993, p. 3).

Fitzgerald's approach to the construction of his narrator was articulated in a September 1939 letter to Kenneth Littauer, in which he writes that Cecelia "is *of* the movies but not *in* them" (Fitzgerald 1994, p. 409) positioning her as "within and without" of the narrative in a similar manner to Nick Carraway (Fitzgerald 2019, p. 43). He also indicates that his intention was to separate the events from the narrating of them. Cecelia "was twenty when the events that she tells occurred, but she is twenty-five when she tells about the events, and of course many of them appear to her in a different light" (Fitzgerald 1994, p. 409). This is another indication that Fitzgerald was drawing upon his narrative technique in *The Great Gatsby*, where he exploited the gap between Nick Carraway's response to the events as they occurred and his views on those same events at the time of narrating the story. The artistic success of *Gatsby* was clearly on his mind as he approached this new work as he makes a comparison between *Tycoon* and his previous novels:

> There's nothing that worries me in the novel, nothing that seems uncertain. Unlike *Tender Is the Night* it is not the story of deterioration—it is not depressing and not morbid in spite of the tragic ending. If one book could ever be "like" another I should say it is more "like" *The Great Gatsby* than any other of my books. But I hope it will be entirely different—I hope it will be something new, arouse new emotions perhaps even a new way of looking at certain phenomena. (Fitzgerald 1994, p. 412)

In this letter, Fitzgerald is pointing to a change—if not in subject matter, then in focus in this novel compared to his previous ones. The hero of *Tycoon*, Monroe Stahr, is a man at the height of his powers and success. Fitzgerald presents a man who is dedicated to his vocation and undistracted by the trappings of money that have blinded his other protagonists. In all of his novels, Fitzgerald was preoccupied with the idea of meaningful work, but this indicates a change of direction. In previous novels the hero is either trying to identify his vocation (*This Side of Paradise, The Beautiful and Damned*), misunderstanding it (*The Great Gatsby*), or betraying it (*Tender Is the Night*). Finally, in this novel Fitzgerald was ready to depict a man dedicated to his vocation.

Fitzgerald modeled his hero on film producer Irving Thalberg (1899–1937), a Hollywood wunderkind who was noted for his ability to produce and maintain high-quality pictures that were commercially successful. No doubt, Fitzgerald was impressed by this balancing act that he himself had managed at the beginning of his career even if he had not been able to maintain it throughout it. What is interesting in his choice of hero is that Stahr comes from a class of people that was a source of some irritation to the novelist who felt that studio executives did not appreciate his talents or make use of them effectively. However, perhaps it was his recognition that the collaborative nature of cinema needed a different kind of visionary from the art of a previous age. Thalberg and Stahr are conduits who channel the brilliance of others in the creation of a project that required a multitude of different talents as well as an enormous amount of money.

It is impossible to say how much of the published *The Last Tycoon* would have remained unchanged had Fitzgerald lived to complete his novel. There even remains an ongoing discussion as to what is the correct title for the novel. In the Cambridge editions of Fitzgerald's work, which are seen as definitive, it is called *The Love of the Last Tycoon: A Western*. This, however, is controversial. There are indications that the book may well have been a success even if there were obstacles in terms of plot and theme that Fitzgerald still needed to overcome. What can be said with certainty is that what we do have of the novel demonstrates a recommitment on the part of Fitzgerald to his vocation, a rededication of himself to his great talent and its expression.

FURTHER READING

Blazek, W., and L. Rattray. 2007. *Twenty-First Century Readings of* Tender Is the Night. Liverpool: Liverpool University Press.

Kroll Ring, F. 1985. *Against the Current: As I Remember F. Scott Fitzgerald*. Berkeley: Creative Arts Book Company.

Schulberg, B. 1993. *The Disenchanted*. London: Allison & Busby.

Stern, M. 1994. *Tender Is the Night: The Broken Universe*. New York: Twayne Publishers.

FURTHER VIEWING

Bromell, H., dir. *Last Call*. 2002. Culver City, CA: Sonar Entertainment.

Miller, L., J. West, E. Templeton, K. Curnutt, R. S. Williams, and R. Webb. "Gatsby in Connecticut: *Tender Is the Night*." 2020 Pandemic Fitzgerald Webinar Series. Webinar from ATG Communications, September 18, 2020. https://vimeo.com/462029771.

Ray, B., dir. *The Last Tycoon*. 2017. Santa Monica, CA: Amazon Studios.

Chapter 6
Short Stories and Essays

To try to do justice in a brief chapter to the number of stories and essays written by Fitzgerald through the course of his twenty-year career is not possible. His short stories number close to two hundred and Fitzgerald wrote dozens of essays, public letters, and magazine articles. Too often, he is a writer reduced to one outstanding novel in *The Great Gatsby*, but a closer look at not only his other novels but his short stories and essays reveals a man who consistently produced high-quality work throughout his career. Part of the misconception was created by Fitzgerald himself who, throughout his working life, belittled his commercial fiction largely because he felt it kept him away from his true vocation of novelist. What follows is therefore a consideration of some of his most significant stories and essays.

SHORT STORIES

F. Scott Fitzgerald's career as a short story writer began at the same time as his career as a novelist. On the advice of the now largely forgotten novelist Grace Flandrau, Fitzgerald contacted the Paul Revere Reynolds Agency in October 1919 in the hope that they would agree to sell his shorter fiction to the lucrative magazine market. He was assigned Harold Ober as his agent and so began a relationship that would last to the end of his life. Indeed, when Ober set up his own agency in 1929, Fitzgerald followed him. His short stories were the mainstay of his income throughout his career; the quality varied but there are some masterful examples of the genre. Key themes that reappear in Fitzgerald's stories are courtship and marriage, youth, Americans in Europe, the contrast between the North and the South, and Hollywood.

"The Ice Palace" (1920)

This early story introduces a number of the themes that Fitzgerald would explore throughout his career. It tells the story of southern belle Sally Carol Happer who lives in the fictional town of Tarleton, Georgia, which was based on Zelda's Montgomery, Alabama. Sally falls in love and becomes engaged to Northerner Harry Bellamy. She travels north and almost freezes to death in an ice palace at a winter carnival. The experience leads her to break the engagement and return to the South.

The story explores the contrast between the two regions of the United States that Fitzgerald was fascinated by throughout his life and demonstrates his ambivalence to the South to which he was both attracted and repelled. It is presented as indolent, lazy, warm, and romantic, whereas the North is shown as industrious, practical, and active.

The other stories in the Tarleton series are "The Jelly-Bean" (1920) and "The Last of the Belles" (1928). "The Ice Palace" was published in *The Saturday Evening Post* on May 22, 1920.

"May Day" (1920)

"May Day" is an unusual story in the Fitzgerald canon for a number of reasons. First, it has an overtly political backdrop that draws upon the May Day Riots of 1919. It involves an antisocialist march, newly demobilized soldiers, a radical newspaper, and a riot. Second, it is noteworthy that Fitzgerald explores the lives and experiences of working-class characters in the form of discharged soldiers, Carroll Key and Gus Rose. They will be part of the antisocialist riot that will involve attacking the offices of a radical newspaper. Alongside the storyline of the riots is the fate of Gordon Sterrett, a man rapidly deteriorating much to the disgust of his wealthy Yale classmate, Philip Dean. He is being blackmailed by his working-class girlfriend, Jewel Hudson, while still being in love with his prewar sweetheart, Edith Bradin. She has been preoccupied with memories of Sterrett but when they are reunited she is disenchanted. Sterrett gets drunk and wakes the next morning not only hungover but married to Jewel. He buys a gun and kills himself.

The story explores some of Fitzgerald's favorite themes: love, disillusionment, and deterioration. Sterrett's suicide, however, also brings into sharp focus that as an author Fitzgerald was not afraid to contend with complex and painful themes; he was not simply the writer of flapper tales.

The story, along with *The Beautiful and Damned*, shows the influence of literary critic and proponent of naturalism, H. L. Mencken (1880–1956). Emerging out of Realism, Naturalism was a literary style (and philosophical movement) that was concerned with presenting human experience as subject to forces beyond human control. Humanity is part of nature and subject to its laws and causes and is not interfered with by supernatural or spiritual forces.

The story was published in *The Smart Set*, a magazine edited by Mencken himself and another of Fitzgerald's friends, George Jean Nathan (1882–1958). The publication printed stories by a wealth of new and upcoming writers during its 1920s heyday. "May Day" was published in July 1920. In Fitzgerald's introduction to his collection of short stories *Tales of the Jazz Age* (1922), which included "May Day," he asserted that the "hysteria around the events of Spring 1919 had "inaugurated the Age of Jazz" (Fitzgerald 2002, p. 6).

"Winter Dreams" (1922)

"Winter Dreams" tells the story of Dexter Green's love for Judy Jones, a woman very much in the vein of the golden girl best represented in Fitzgerald's work by Daisy Fay Buchanan. Indeed, the story has been seen as an early model for the love story of Daisy and Gatsby. The events take place over an extended period of time and chart Dexter's love for the wealthy and emotionally self-ish Judy. The story makes use of one of Fitzgerald's favorite plot lines as the middle-class Dexter pursues the wealthy Judy whom he meets while caddying at a golf club. He quits his job rather than be in the position of servitude toward her. Dexter attends college and becomes financially successful and returns home where he once again meets Judy, and a relationship develops between them. However, Dexter discovers that he is one among Judy's many beaus. He becomes engaged to another woman but ends that relationship when Judy renews her interest in him. They become engaged but Judy breaks the engage-ment after a month.

Seven years later Dexter is living in New York and has not returned home. He is told by a business acquaintance that Judy is married to a friend of his who treats her poorly. Her much admired good looks have also faded. Dexter, still in love with Judy, realizes that his dream is dead, and his illusions are shattered. He realizes that a return home is now impossible.

This brief summary makes clear the links the story has to *The Great Gatsby* both thematically and in terms of plot. It is also possible to see Fitzgerald drawing upon his own experience of his broken engagement with Zelda as well as his rejection by his first love, the wealthy and beautiful Ginevra King. Fitzger-ald's depiction of desire, loss, and disillusionment in this story has the same wistful quality so beautifully created in *Gatsby*.

"Winter Dreams" was published in *Metropolitan* magazine in their 1922 December issue. It was included in Fitzgerald's short story collection *All the Sad Young Men* (1926) alongside another of the *Gatsby* cluster of stories, "Absolu-tion," originally published in the June 1924 edition of *American Mercury*.

"Jacob's Ladder" (1927)

The significance of "Jacob's Ladder" is twofold. First, it points toward *Tender Is the Night* in its depiction of a relationship between a younger female and an older man. Jacob—just like Dick Diver—is drawn to the innocence of an adoles-cent on the verge of the adult world. However, both become despondent and saddened as the objects of their affection enter womanhood. Second, this story is set in the film industry and was published in the same year as Fitzgerald's first stint in Hollywood. Fitzgerald would also make use of his understanding of the movies and the women working in them in his creation of starlet Rosemary Hoyt in *Tender Is the Night.*

Jacob Booth, a 33-year-old man, meets Jenny Delehanty, a 16-year-old shop girl, in the aftermath of her sister's trial for murder. She changes her name to Jenny Prince and Jacob introduces her to a film director, Billy Farrelly, who offers her a leading role in one of his pictures. Subsequently, she is offered a contract and leaves New York for Hollywood. Jenny welcomes the opportunity but is sad to be separated from Jacob. Six months later, Jacob—who is now in love with her—visits her and realizes that she is no longer the innocent he had known previously. He is unhappy about the attention she attracts from other men. He tells Jenny about his love for her, but she rejects him. After rescuing her from a blackmail plot involving her sister, Jacob asks Jenny to marry him, but she refuses as she plans to marry the director of her latest film. After they have parted, he goes to a movie theater to watch her latest picture in an attempt to recapture the girl he had once known. The story was published for the first time on August 27, 1927, in *The Saturday Evening Post.*

"The Last of the Belles" (1929)

This story—set in Tarleton, Georgia, a fictional re-creation of Montgomery, Alabama—tells the story of Ailie Calhoun through the eyes of Andy and told retrospectively. During the First World War, Andy is stationed in an army camp near the town and becomes a confidant of Ailie. He witnesses her pursuit by a number of men, including Bill Knowles and Horace Canby. Canby is an aviator who crashes his plane when Knowles returns on leave from Texas and reunites with Ailie. The relationship with Knowles also fizzles out after he makes an ultimatum that she rejects. Earl Shoen is another of Ailie's beaus, but she breaks it off with him too. In the aftermath of the war and without his uniform, the illusion of what she thought he was is broken. He returns to his native North as does Andy.

Some years later Andy returns to Tarleton and reunites with Ailie, aware that he has been in love with her all along. She asserts that she could never marry a Northern man and instead is engaged to wed a gentleman from Savannah. At the end of the story the pair head out to the site of the army camp. Andy reflects that, for him, after Ailie's marriage the "South would be empty [. . .] forever" (Fitzgerald 1989, p. 463). It was first published in the March 2, 1929, edition of *The Saturday Evening Post.*

"Babylon Revisited" (1931)

"Babylon Revisited" tells the story of Charlie Wales, who having lived in Paris during the boom years returns to the city in 1930. His first stop is a previous haunt, the Ritz Bar, where he inquires after old acquaintances and leaves his sister-in-law's address for his friend, Duncan Schaeffer. He then visits the home of his in-laws with whom his daughter, Honoria, lives. It is revealed that Wales is limiting himself to one drink a day after the excesses of the previous decade had led to dissipation and waste. After leaving the couple's home, he visits a series of places he frequented in the 1920s and reflects on the period and its excesses.

The next day, while having lunch with his daughter, he bumps into the Schaeffers but, in light of his reflections of the previous evening and his desire to regain custody of Honoria, he does not give them his address. He speaks to his sister-in-law, Marion, about the purpose of his visit and—during this conversation—it is revealed to the reader that after a drunken argument with his wife, Helen, he locked her outside in the snow, which contributed to her premature death. Marion is unwilling to relinquish guardianship of Honoria to which Charlie had agreed while receiving treatment in a sanatorium. However, Marion's husband, Lincoln, is open to the prospect of returning Honoria to her father.

The following evening Charlie is at Marion and Lincoln's home when the Schaeffers show up drunk. Charlie sends them away but Marion, already opposed to Honoria returning to the care of her father, is horrified and determines that she will retain custody for a further six months. Charlie returns to the Ritz Bar and reflects on how much he lost during the expatriate Boom years of the 1920s.

"Babylon Revisited" is considered one of Fitzgerald's most brilliant stories. The text explores the decadence of the 1920s and the expatriate life but also the financial and emotional price paid for excesses of the decade. There are aspects of Fitzgerald's life seeping into the story, particularly in Charlie's guilt about his dead wife. The story was written less than a year after Zelda's mental collapse that—at times—Fitzgerald felt he had a role in triggering. The story also touches on Charlie's problematic relationship with alcohol, although the suggestion is that limiting oneself to a drink a day could sufficiently rectify the devastating consequences of full-blown alcoholism.

Even in fiction, Fitzgerald found it difficult to depict—or even fathom—complete abstinence. The story was published in *The Saturday Evening Post* on February 21, 1931.

ESSAYS

Fitzgerald's essays of the 1920s often have a light-hearted, humorous undercurrent. They can be tongue-in-cheek or play on Fitzgerald's public persona by exceeding the reader's expectations of his notoriety. However, there are also reflections on the cultural moment and his own changing life and circumstances. In "What I Think and Feel at 25" (1922), for example, he reflects on the responsibilities and anxieties that come with marriage and fatherhood. He also explores the growing generation gap, playing on his image as the voice of America's youth.

In "Imagination and a Few Mothers" (1923), Fitzgerald contrasts a nervous and anxious mother with a woman of exceptional grace and charm. It is a comical essay, but with knowledge of Fitzgerald's complex relationship with his own mother it takes on not only a gravitas not initially evident, but also a mood of profound sadness.

"How to Live on $36,000 a Year" (1924) and "How to Live on Practically Nothing a Year" (1924) comically explore the Fitzgeralds' complex relationship with money. In the first essay, Fitzgerald describes the financial irresponsibility of himself and his wife while living in New York and Great Neck in 1923. It repeatedly asks the question, where is their money disappearing to? This humorous piece takes on a more serious tone when viewed through the lens of Fitzgerald's desperate financial situation in the 1930s. The accompanying essay is an amusing account of the couple trying—and failing—to economize on the French Riviera when they headed to Europe in 1924.

During the difficult decade of the 1930s, Fitzgerald's essays took on a somber, melancholy, and nostalgic tone. In "Echoes of the Jazz Age" (1931), he reflects on the excesses of the carefree 1920s as the product of the chaotic, unspent energy generated by the First World War. He then charts the degeneration that was the aftermath of the decade into the social, mental, and financial collapse of the 1930s. The essay's poignancy is exacerbated with the realization that Fitzgerald's personal life echoed the plight of the nation.

In "My Lost City" (1935), the author explores his changing emotional engagement with New York. The city was an environment of triumph, excitement, and optimism during the early part of his career, but morphed into a heartbreaking symbol of loss, regret, and nostalgia.

In "The Crack-Up" (1936) and the essays that followed in the series for *Esquire*, Fitzgerald charted his own emotional collapse, the result of the emotional, psychological, and creative battering he had received through the early to mid-1930s. The publication only seemed to attract further negative attention from the public and peers alike. However, the honesty of a man struggling with circumstances that were both within and beyond his control is poignant. For a modern audience, more comfortable with emotional and psychological vulnerabilities, they are powerful examples of a man confronting himself. That said, Fitzgerald seemed unable to fully admit the disastrous impact that alcohol had had on both his personal and professional life. However, the denial, in some respects, only adds to the poignancy of the essays.

Fitzgerald's essays from throughout his career as well as his letters deserve more attention both in terms of their own artistry but also as important examples of Fitzgerald engaging with—and revealing—the society in which he lived.

FURTHER READING

Broughton Adams, J. 2020. *F. Scott Fitzgerald's Short Fiction: From Ragtime to Swing Time*. Edinburgh: Edinburgh University Press.

Bryer, J., ed. 1982. *The Short Stories of F. Scott Fitzgerald: New Approaches in Criticism*. Madison: University of Wisconsin Press.

Fitzgerald, F. S. 2005. *My Lost City: Personal Essays 1920–1940*. Cambridge: Cambridge University Press.

Fitzgerald, F. S. 2013. *The Lost Decade: Short Stories from Esquire, 1936–1941*. Cambridge: Cambridge University Press.

Fitzgerald, F. S. 2014. *Taps at Reveille*. Cambridge: Cambridge University Press.

Fitzgerald, F. S. 2017. *I'd Die For You and Other Lost Stories*. London: Scribner.

Hall Petry, A. 1989. *Fitzgerald's Craft of Short Fiction: The Collected Stories 1920–1935*. Tuscaloosa: The University of Alabama Press.

FURTHER VIEWING

Daniel, A. M., B. Mangum, J. Nolan, K. Curnutt, and R. S. Williams. "Gatsby in Connecticut: The Short Stories." 2020 Pandemic Fitzgerald Webinar Series. Webinar from ATG Communications, December 18, 2020. https://vimeo.com/492853989.

FURTHER LISTENING

Curnutt, K., and R. Trogdon. Master the 40: The Stories of F. Scott Fitzgerald. Podcast audio. August 1, 2020. https://www.listennotes.com/podcasts/master-the-40-the-stories-of-f-scott-e3CZpXbn0RB/.

Conclusion

In a remarkable twenty-year career, F. Scott Fitzgerald produced five novels (one unfinished), close to two hundred stories, and a large number of essays and magazine articles. It is easy to lose sight of this because of the remarkable shadow that *The Great Gatsby* casts over Fitzgerald's work and American Letters more generally. However, to fully appreciate his masterpiece and his contribution to twentieth-century literature, it is important to engage with and appreciate the rest of his work. The intention of this guide was to provide a useful overview of Fitzgerald's life and work and—in the process—encourage readers to investigate further this extraordinary man and his extraordinary work.

Bibliography

Adams, J. T. 2012. *The Epic of America.* New Brunswick, NJ: Transaction
   Publishers

Bate, J. 2021. *Bright Star, Green Light: The Beautiful Works and the Damned Lives
   of John Keats and F. Scott Fitzgerald.* London: William Collins.

Berman, R. 1994. *The Great Gatsby and Modern Times.* Urbana: University of
   Illinois Press.

Berman, R. 2009. *Translating Modernism: Fitzgerald and Hemingway.* Tuscaloosa:
   The University of Alabama Press.

Blazek, W., and L. Rattray, eds. 2007. *Twenty-First Century Readings of* Tender
   Is the Night. Liverpool: Liverpool University Press.

Broughton Adams, J. 2020. *F. Scott Fitzgerald's Short Fiction: From Ragtime to
   Swingtime.* Edinburgh: Edinburgh University Press.

Brown, D. S. 2017. *Paradise Lost: A Life of F. Scott Fitzgerald.* Cambridge, MA:
   The Belknap Press of Harvard University Press.

Bruccoli, M. J. 1963. *The Composition of* Tender Is the Night. Pittsburgh: University of Pittsburgh Press.

Bruccoli, M. J. 2002. *Some Sort of Epic Grandeur: The Life of F. Scott Fitzgerald,*
   2nd rev. ed. Columbia: University of South Carolina Press .

Bruccoli, M. J., and G. P. Anderson, eds. 2003. *F. Scott Fitzgerald's* Tender Is the
   Night: *A Documentary Volume.* Farmington Hills, MI: Thomson Gale.

Bruccoli, M. J., and J. S. Baughman, eds. 2004. *The Sons of Maxwell Perkins:
   Letters of F. Scott Fitzgerald, Ernest Hemingway, Thomas Wolfe, and Their
   Editor.* Columbia: University of South Carolina Press.

Bryer, J., ed. 1982. *The Short Stories of F. Scott Fitzgerald: New Approaches in
   Criticism.* Madison: University of Wisconsin Press.

Churchwell, S. 2014. *Careless People: Murder, Mayhem and the Invention of* The
   Great Gatsby. London: Virago.

Curnutt, K., ed. 2004. *A Historical Guide to F. Scott Fitzgerald.* New York: Oxford
   University Press.

Curnutt, K. 2007. *The Cambridge Introduction to F. Scott Fitzgerald*. Cambridge: Cambridge University Press.

Donaldson, S. 2012. *F. Scott Fitzgerald: Fool for Love*. Minneapolis: University of Minnesota Press.

Eliot, T. S. 2009. *The Letters of T. S. Eliot. Vol. 2: 1923–1925*. London: Faber and Faber.

Fine, R. 2013. "The Writer in Hollywood." In *F. Scott Fitzgerald in Context*, edited by B. Mangum, 388–99. New York: Cambridge University Press.

Fitzgerald, F. S. 1989. *The Short Stories of F. Scott Fitzgerald*. London: Abacus.

Fitzgerald, F. S. 1993. *The Love of the Last Tycoon: A Western*. Cambridge: Cambridge University Press.

Fitzgerald, F. S. 1994. *A Life in Letters: F Scott Fitzgerald*. New York: Charles Scribner's Sons.

Fitzgerald, F. S. 2000. *Trimalchio: An Early Version of The Great Gatsby*. Cambridge: Cambridge University Press.

Fitzgerald, F. S. 2002. *Tales of the Jazz Age*. Cambridge: Cambridge University Press.

Fitzgerald, F. S. 2005. *My Lost City: Personal Essays 1920–1940*. Cambridge: Cambridge University Press.

Fitzgerald, F. S. 2008. *The Beautiful and Damned*. Cambridge: University of Cambridge Press.

Fitzgerald, F. S. 2012a. *Tender Is the Night*. Cambridge: Cambridge University Press.

Fitzgerald, F. S. 2012b. *This Side of Paradise*. Cambridge: Cambridge University Press.

Fitzgerald, F. S. 2013. *The Lost Decade: Short Stories from Esquire, 1936–1941*. Cambridge: Cambridge University Press.

Fitzgerald, F. S. 2014. *Taps at Reveille*. Cambridge: Cambridge University Press.

Fitzgerald, F. S. 2017. *I'd Die For You and Other Lost Stories*. London: Scribner.

Fitzgerald, F. S. 2019. *The Great Gatsby: A Variorum Edition*. Cambridge: Cambridge University Press.

Hall Petry, A. 1989. *Fitzgerald's Craft of Short Fiction: The Collected Stories 1920–1935*. Tuscaloosa: The University of Alabama Press.

Hemingway, E. 1994. *A Moveable Feast*. London: Arrow Books.

Kroll Ring, F. 1985. *Against the Current: As I Remember F. Scott Fitzgerald*. Berkeley: Creative Arts Book Company.

Latham, A. 1972. *Crazy Sundays: F. Scott Fitzgerald in Hollywood.* London: Secker & Warburg.

Long, R. 1979. *The Achieving of* The Great Gatsby: *F. Scott Fitzgerald, 1920–1925.* Lewisburg, Pa.: Bucknell University Press.

Mangum, B., ed. 2013. *F. Scott Fitzgerald in Context.* New York: Cambridge University Press.

Prigozy, R., ed. 2002. *The Cambridge Companion to F. Scott Fitzgerald.* Cambridge: Cambridge University Press.

Schulberg, B. 1993. *The Disenchanted.* London: Allison & Busby.

Stern, M. 1994. *Tender Is the Night: The Broken Universe.* New York: Twayne Publishers.

Tate, M. J. 1998. *F. Scott Fitzgerald A–Z: The Essential Reference to His Life and Work.* New York: Checkmark Books.

Vaill, A. 1998. *Everybody Was So Young: Gerald and Sara Murphy: A Lost Generation Love Story.* London: Little, Brown and Company.

West, J. L. W., III. 1983. *The Making of* This Side of Paradise. Philadelphia: University of Pennsylvania Press.

Wilson, E., ed. 1945. *The Crack-Up.* New York: New Directions.

Index